The Melancholy of Departure

Winner of
The Flannery O'Connor Award
for Short Fiction

The Melancholy of Departure

Stories by Alfred DePew

The University of Georgia Press

Athens & London

© 1992 by Alfred DePew

Published by the University of Georgia Press
Athens, Georgia 30602
Designed by Louise M. Jones
Set in 11/15 Fournier by Tseng Information Systems, Inc.
Printed and bound by Braun-Brumfield
The paper in this book meets the guidelines for
permanence and durability of the Committee on
Production Guidelines for Book Longevity of the
Council on Library Resources.

Printed in the United States of America

96   95   94   93   92   C   5   4   3   2   1

Library of Congress Cataloging in Publication Data

DePew, Alfred.
The melancholy of departure :
stories / by Alfred DePew. p.   cm.
ISBN 0-8203-1405-6 (alk. paper)
1. Title.
PS3554.E1148M45   1992
813'.54—dc20   91-24281
                              CIP

British Library Cataloging in Publication Data available

"At Home with the Pelletiers"
was previously published in *Tallinn*.

For Don Murray
and Dianne Benedict
who bore witness.

And for Myra Black
because I promised.

The publication of this book
is supported by a grant from the
National Endowment for the Arts,
a federal agency.

Contents

The Melancholy of Departure

Let Me Tell You How
I Met My First Husband,
the Clown

*n*o really. That's what he does for work. And you already
guessed. I was in the audience. I wasn't even going to go,
but my friend Sylvia said, "Come on, you study too much,
we're going." In those days I was very serious. I was going to
be an actress. Very serious. The only part I wanted to play was
Medea. I figured there was a woman with spine. Lady Macbeth
wasn't bad either, but she was too snooty. For me, nothing would
do but the Greeks. Shakespeare was a little messy—all those
bodies onstage at the end of *Hamlet*. Who could believe it? No. I
preferred my murders offstage. That way nothing would detract
from my lines. I'm telling you, those Greeks had class. Besides,
what could I possibly learn from a clown?

But Sylvia said, "Come on," so I grabbed my coat, and we
trudged through the Wisconsin snow to the college chapel to
watch this guy. I was determined not to laugh. I was hell-bent to
not even enjoy it a little. Laugh? Not on your life. And the audience! Philistines, every one. This was kid stuff, and at nineteen I
was not a kid. Now, the older I get . . . well. But middle age is
another story. This is how we met.

He was tall and skinny. I mean skinny. And he had this sharp nose, very Anglican-looking or Presbyterian or something. Whatever. In the Midwest, everyone looks the same—not like anybody I knew growing up in Manhattan. They look like everybody on TV who isn't Jewish or Italian, like they've got this special farm in Iowa maybe to breed them. So he looked like that, like he sprouted up from the earth between two cornstalks in a field outside Normal, Illinois, though he was in reality from Beardsville, which, after I got to know him, I called Weirdsville. He said it was my Jewish wit. You should have seen his mother's face when she met me. But that came later.

This night, I sat in the way back because I knew he'd probably pull people out of the first rows and bring them up onstage, and I'd have died. A serious actress like myself, sharing the spotlight with a guy who did circus tricks. So I sat there, determined not to laugh, and he did his first thing, which was not so bad actually. I could see the humor in it. I could see why the audience liked him. They were not what you'd call sophisticated. What I'm saying is it was a certain *kind* of humor, the kind of thing you've seen a thousand times—Emmett Kelly stuff, the stuff Red Skelton does, good for what it is, but a little thin in intellectual content. If you don't know what I'm talking about, I can't explain it.

The thing is he was kind of beautiful, his eyes and his long, long fingers. And he was a good mime too. I had to hand him that. He made all the invisible walls and shelves and ropes seem very real. I wondered if he had studied in Paris, which would have redeemed him a little in my mind. Then he did this thing about a baseball game, he was completely different for every player, and I confess I laughed a little. Though, you live in the heartland a year or two, you begin to get some of the jokes—real cornball stuff. It catches you off guard, you have a little affection for it, but I was still determined not to give in to him. And you know? It's as if he knew that, and I swear he began playing right to me. He had these blue, blue eyes (cornflower blue, his mother called them; I always found that nauseating—I always found *her* nauseating, and believe me, the feeling was mutual, though she was too nice to admit it, but of course nice had nothing to do with it; she was a liar, a very dishonest person with her emotions).

Anyway, I noticed him looking at me straight and stern, with this big grin every time he turned towards my part of the audience. And the more I didn't laugh, the more he sort of bore down on me, grinning. I swear he could see me, even though I was so far away, and to tell you the truth, it made me very nervous because I knew he was working up to the part of his schtick when he pulls innocent people up on the stage, and I was getting self-conscious, like other people knew he was playing to me, and it occurred to me that he might be crazy enough to do something that would embarrass me in public.

He did these little magic tricks—you know, the forty-seven Ping-Pong balls that keep coming out of his mouth and his sleeves and his coat pockets? And then it happened. He pointed to someone in the first row, and a little blonde coed (I hate the term to this day, but if it fits) flounced up on the stage and started to giggle. He did everything she did, put his hand over his mouth, toed the floor, shooed her away. Then he handed her his cane and tried to teach her how to balance it on her nose, which of course got a big laugh. Then he took it back from her and made like it got very heavy all of a sudden—you know the trick—like it was a barbell, and he picked it up, raised it to just under his chin, and then sank under its weight until he fell back, hard, like it had pinned him to the floor. He stuck out his hand, and the little coed grabbed it and pulled him up.

That's when I noticed I wanted to kill her. My hands were clutching the arms of my seat, and I hoisted myself up a little.

Sylvia leaned over and said, "What's the matter?" and I sat back down again. I was breathing hard. I stared straight out in front of me, and Sylvia rightly took that to mean: Don't ask any questions, I'll explain it later. Which I did. In fact, I spent years trying to explain it to Sylvia, who always listened angelically but I think never understood. How could she? I didn't understand it myself.

I wanted to pull that coed's hair out by the handful, and I remember thinking there was probably more of it all wound up in her head; her skull was full of it, like that doll, Tressy. It was a waking nightmare. As if everything surrounding that man was rigged somehow. And then the strangest thing happened; I wanted to kill him too—for making me feel like a fool, for pulling reality out from under me.

You can see why Medea held such a fascination for me in those days. We had the same problem. We tended to overreact.

By intermission I was beside myself. I ran to the ladies' room, locked myself in a stall, and wept. When I got back to my seat, I could tell Sylvia was edgy. She was dying to know. "Do you want to leave?" she said. "Not on your life," I said. And I laughed and cried all through the second half.

I didn't go up to him right after. I had my pride. I knew I had to talk to him, but I couldn't figure out a way. I asked someone, "Hey, where does he go next?" And the answer was Rockford College in Rockford, Illinois, which was not so very far away I couldn't borrow a car and drive there.

So that's what I did. I kept trying to figure out what I was going to do once I got there, because after the performance, it would be the same. People would go up to him to tell him they enjoyed it and maybe flirt with him a little, and I didn't want to be one of them. I wanted to be set apart, noticed a little apart.

Sylvia lent me her old Ford Falcon, which until the day I borrowed it had been very dependable and never any trouble to Sylvia or anybody else. And the motor was fine. It was the tire that was shot. Bam! It blew right after I got beyond the outskirts of Madison, too far to walk back, so I stood there, waving my arms at passing cars.

I'm embarrassed to admit that at nineteen I did not yet know how to change a flat tire. But then how would I learn? It's not a skill you need when you ride the subway. So I'm trying to flag down a passing motorist when this van drives by, and right off I recognize Danny. He flashes me that big grin with an expression of sympathy on his face that could melt iron. Then he shrugs his shoulders—both hands off the steering wheel—points to his watch, and drives on. I was too stunned to even give him the finger. I stomped back to the Falcon and kicked one of the tires that still had air in it. Pretty soon, someone stopped and changed the tire. Thank God Sylvia had a spare that was OK. She was and still is I bet a very cautious and thorough person. And smart too. When she was a second-semester junior, she saw the writing on the wall. She changed her major from ethnomusicology to bookkeeping, which she could fall back on when her marriage to the dentist in Chicago didn't work out. He used to beat her up. How could she have known? He always seemed very gentle; he never raised his voice. When I knew him, he wore African shirts and sandals and clover chains around his neck. Remember the new sensitivity young men were cultivating in those days? It was a cruel joke. But what did we know? We thought we could end the war in Southeast Asia in six weeks. We thought marijuana would change the world. You have to understand: we were only kids.

About twenty miles down the road, I saw this van pulled over and a man stooped down, peering into the engine in the back. I knew right away it was him, even before I could see "Daniel Muldoon: One-Man Flying Circus" painted on the side panel. What luck! When I hopped out of the car, I shouted, "That'll teach you to drive past a woman stranded by the side of the road." And this surprised me. Believe it or not, I was a shy girl in those days.

Sure, now—I see a man I like, and well, it's a different story. But then it was unusual for me to be so brash right off; I would wait until I got to know a person a little.

Danny grinned again. He looked like he was glad to see me. And not just because I stopped. He knew how to fix the van himself; it must have broken down thirty times in the seven years we were together, and he always fixed it himself. "Here," he said, "hold the flashlight."

So I held the flashlight while he banged around inside the motor with his monkey wrench. Pretty soon, he asked where I was headed.

"Rockford," I said.

"What do you know," he said. "That's where I'm going."

"No kidding," I said.

"Yeah," he said. "I've got a show at the college there tonight. You should come see it—as my guest."

"Sure," I said. "I'd like that."

"What do you do?" he asked.

"Medea," I said.

"How's that?" He pulled his head from under the hood and gave me a quizzical look.

"I'm an actress," I said. "Classical. I'm a Greek Jew, and the Greeks, I don't know, they kind of get to me. You know what I mean?"

When I saw how impressed he was, I was ashamed for having lied. My grandparents on both sides were Lithuanian. I don't know what got into me to say I was Greek. To a farm boy, what's the difference? Chicago is exotic. Why split hairs between Greece and Lithuania? But it was important right off he should know I come from people with a heritage, even though, looking back, I was taking the first step in my life that would cut me off from it.

We were married three days later in Evanston. Well, married.

I should explain. It was not the sort of marriage a judge would recognize as legal, but if we hadn't moved from state to state so much, it would have been a common-law marriage. Maybe it was. I don't know if there's a federal law. I always meant to look that up. Legal or not, and I mean this, I felt more married to Danny than I did to any of the men I have subsequently married at the justice of the peace or in a Unitarian church or even in a synagogue with the in-laws there and a cantor and a bouquet.

It was the first, last, and only time we were onstage together. I sat in the front row, and when it came time for him to pull someone out of the audience, he chose me. I resisted at first, then I gave in, and once I was up there, what could I do, I was an actress; I tried not to look too stupid while he blew up balloons and twisted them into shapes. I played with him. I took the heart he made, put my arm through it, pointed to my sleeve, put it on my head, wore it like a crown. It was like nothing I'd ever done onstage. I lost all awareness of myself and the audience. I felt light as air, full of a shining beauty.

He stood erect and grim and fierce in front of me, with his hands open like he was holding a book; then he stood at my side, all bashful, shifting from one foot to the other, looking down at me and then away and then back again. Then he was the preacher again, and then the bridegroom.

Before I knew it, he slipped a balloon ring onto my wrist and played the wedding recessional on a kazoo as he marched me around the stage with everyone laughing and clapping. Then he stopped. He kissed me, and I had clown white all around my mouth. He raised his hands, came out of character and announced: "Ladies and gentlemen, I'd like you to meet Mrs. Daniel Muldoon." The audience stood up. They actually stood up and cheered, and I could see some of the women were dabbing their eyes with handkerchiefs. I remember thinking: They wish they were me; they wish they were going to have the life I'm going to have. And it was then I knew not one of them could take that away from me.

The next morning we drove back to Madison to return Sylvia's car, and that same day I packed everything I could fit in the van and told Sylvia to sell the rest. "Are you crazy?" she said, "What about exams?"

"Sylvia," I said, "exams I can take anytime. Following the man I love to the ends of the earth is a once-in-a-lifetime opportunity." Or so I thought. What did I know?

As practical as Sylvia is, I think she was a little jealous. And lonely to see me drive off with my one-man flying circus. She cried, and she kissed me. She made Danny promise to take good care of me. She stood on the curb, waving, and then made me get out of the van to hug her again. She said, "Good luck, be happy, keep in touch, be careful, and don't worry, I'll sell everything and send you the money," which she did. And then she cried again. Sweet Sylvia. My best friend in this life.

But before I left Madison, I had to call home. I couldn't just vanish. A Jewish girl disappears in the Midwest, you could find her hanging by the neck from a tree with a note from the Ku Klux Klan pinned to her lapel. So I called and said, "Hi, Ma. Guess what? I'm married. Be happy for me. I'm not pregnant. He's a great actor. We're going on the road. I'll keep in touch. Give my love to Pa. Bye." And I hung up. It was best not to get into a lengthy discussion.

We were on the road for seven years. Which is not to say we never lived in an apartment; we just never settled anywhere too long. Eighteen months in a place was about our limit. We toured big cities, small cities, all the college towns. Sometimes Danny would have to get a job waiting tables, but mostly I worked the money job to leave him free to perform and teach. I never became an actress. At this point, a number of you feminists are grinding your teeth and clenching your fists. But it wasn't like that. Danny never held me back. I lost my passion for Medea; it was no big tragedy. My interests broadened. I discovered politics. Those were the years of the revolution; there was always something you could do. I stuffed envelopes and canvassed neighborhoods and marched and got myself arrested a lot. Once or twice, Danny experimented with guerrilla theater, the stuff they were doing in the streets, but to be perfectly honest, he wasn't very good at it. He never could make himself frightening enough. He just wasn't an angry man; his heart wasn't in it.

And I knitted. I couldn't smoke during the performance, so I would knit. I knitted booties and little sweaters and blankets for the kids his sisters and our friends were having. I knitted us both sweaters and gloves and mittens and socks. Now I can't stand the thought of knitting. I must have gotten it all out of my system. It's too bad; there are times when my little boy needs something, but I figure it's simpler to buy. I don't have the time anymore.

And I watched. I must have seen Danny perform 896 times in the seven years we were together. It's not like it was the same thing all the time. He changed his act a lot, tried out new material, added, deleted, rotated his routines, and he improvised a great deal; it depended on the crowd. I can't say I ever got bored, and it's hard for me to think now what was my favorite. As much as I loved talking to him and fighting with him and watching him sleep and of course making love with him—for that alone, he should've gotten awards—I think I always loved him best when he was onstage. Not best. Maybe different. He was magic. Not altogether of this world.

Every so often, he'd pick a very timid child out of the audience and bring him up on the stage. Without a word, Danny would teach this kid how to do things, little things, something as simple as opening his arms wide and facing the audience, and everybody clapped. I swear you could see this kid changing before your eyes. He'd grin and look up at Danny, like he was beginning to know it was not such a bad thing to be a human being, no matter how little. And in a matter of minutes, Danny would have this kid sit in a chair, get him to hold on tight, and then lift the chair up over his head, hold it with one hand or balance the chair on his chin for a minute—no hands. Nobody would breathe, especially not the kid, and then he'd lower the chair, the kid would hop out— all without a word, mind you—and they'd stand there together, their arms spread wide, both of them grinning, while the crowd clapped and clapped and clapped.

Children loved him. Grown men were spellbound. And women? Well. Women adored him.

I know. You're sitting there very smug, thinking that's why I left him. But you're wrong. I wasn't exactly the most faithful woman on earth either. Face it. The genitals—both male and female—have reasons that reason will never comprehend. Sigmund Freud didn't even figure it out. I left for a lot of reasons. I was getting older. I was tired of traveling. The revolution failed. And believe it or not, I wanted a child by Danny. I terminated two pregnancies—you can't mention the word *abortion* these days without some born-again Nazi trying to lob a grenade into your handbag—Danny and I both decided it wasn't time; there was no money. As I say, we were always on the road. Then when we decided it was time, I miscarried, and after that I began to get sad watching Danny perform, especially when he brought kids on-stage. I grew more and more depressed. It got ugly between us. We said—I said terrible things. God, the look on his face when I told him I was leaving was enough to scorch my heart, but I had to keep saying it, "I'm leaving, no matter what you say or how you look, or how much I love you and want to stay, I'm leaving."

And to tell you the truth, I was homesick. I missed New York. I longed to live in a real neighborhood again and see people every day on the street who looked familiar to me.

So. Well. Here I am. I finished college. I'm a social worker for the city now. I have a son by the husband I married in a synagogue. This husband and I have also parted company. I'm on sabbatical. I needed a break. Marriages, like anything else, can be habit-forming. Besides, I like living alone with my son. He's six and a half. He goes to a good kindergarten run by sensible, progressive people not far from where we live.

I named him Daniel. I told his father it was for a favorite uncle, which was not entirely a lie. My father did have a business associate who was also a friend of the family, and his name was Daniel, but you and I both know who I named my son after. Maybe one day my son will. Who knows? I haven't seen or heard from Daniel Muldoon since I left, and that was thirteen years ago.

The other day I was walking my son home from school. It was my day off, and we passed a guy standing on the corner. He wore a top hat and overalls. He had clown white on his face, and he was doing tricks to make a few bucks. From a distance I saw him and my heart stopped. He was about the same height, almost the same build, but when I got closer I could see he was just a kid, maybe twenty. My son and I stopped at the same moment to watch, without saying a word to each other. Pretty soon my son let go of my hand and made his way to the front of the small group that had gathered. He wanted to get a better look. The guy wearing the top hat motioned him to come forward. He pulled a quarter from behind my son's ear. At first this took my son by surprise, but then because he is already a little skeptical and shows strong tendencies towards serious scientific inquiry, he was looking around for where the quarter *really* came from; in our household, he knows money does not appear out of thin air. The guy pulled another and then another quarter from behind Daniel's ear. My son looked up at me, as if I had the explanation. I looked at him and shrugged.

I thought of Danny Muldoon and the first night I saw him and the look on my son's face a moment earlier. I thought of how hard I had resisted that man when I was nineteen, and how quickly I had fallen in love, of our years together and the nights I watched him perform with a timid child he had pulled from the audience, and how glad and proud that kid looked with his arms spread wide to receive the applause, his face beaming. I thought if only my father had seen that, he might have forgiven me for running off with a Gentile. He might have understood that Daniel Muldoon was not wholly of this world. He might have seen what I now saw, that Danny was a sort of Ba'al Shem Tov with laughing children on his shoulders, a man whom God had put on this earth to show us the study of Talmud was not the only path, God could be worshiped by seeming to make forty-seven Ping-Pong balls appear out of nowhere, and the purpose of living was to make life—all of it—holy.

I closed my eyes and said a little prayer for my father and a little prayer for Danny, that wherever he was he was safe and happy and still working. My son gave my pants leg a tug. "Come on, Mama," he said. "It's over." So I took his hand. It's true, you know, the momentous things in our lives almost always have small beginnings. And we headed home, my son and I, discussing the visible and the invisible, and debating the relative merits of having grilled cheese or sloppy joes for lunch.

Stanley

*S*tanley waits outside your door, wearing neatly creased slacks, a perma-press shirt, and a black beret set squarely on his head. He holds a bunch of roses.

You stand on your side of the door, about to open it. Your living room is a mess. You have just scoured the tub and toilet, swept the bedroom. You have run home from work to get your apartment into some kind of order because you are expecting Stanley, who has told you over the phone that he is a comptroller, and who you guess probably likes order.

But there is nothing to be done now about the living room. You've just bought a two-drawer filing cabinet and pulled it out of its cardboard box. There are papers and letters lying all over the floor, waiting to be filed. You think this filing cabinet is the answer to your life. You are pretty sure, though you have not yet laid eyes on him, that Stanley is not.

You open the door, smile. So this is Stanley. A moment earlier, you half wished he would be physically repulsive. You are suddenly afraid to let desire creep back into your life, and yet you answered his ad in the personal column; you have brought this on yourself.

Right away, you notice the creased slacks, the smooth shirt, the absurd beret. He is holding a dozen peach-colored sweetheart roses, wrapped in green tissue paper. You are struck by how silly he looks standing there.

"So. You must be Stanley."

After shaking hands, you invite him in, and he gives you the roses, which you admire. You are touched; no one has ever brought you roses, but somehow the gesture is all wrong. He looks even sillier inside your apartment than he did in the hallway. Out of context, you think, though you have no idea what his context might be. You imagine an office. You imagine a neat house.

In order that he may sit down, you lift a pile of papers and books off a chair and put it on top of the filing cabinet, which you explain is new and meant to be the answer to your life. As soon as you say this, you wish you had not. You have just admitted to a perfect stranger that your life is something that might need an answer. You have even suggested, unwittingly, that Stanley might be the answer, and you hope he is not thinking this, as you turn to find something to put the roses in.

The only vase you have is too large; it swallows them. You remove them, pour the water out, reenter the living room for a chair to stand on, so that you can reach the top shelf of your kitchen cupboard, where there is a wide-mouthed peanut butter jar. You make conversation with Stanley over your shoulder, as he looks at the postcards, the photographs, the theater posters on your wall, the books in the bookcase you have fashioned from stolen milk crates and planks from an old fence. You really ought to have something better than a peanut butter jar for the roses, but nothing else is the right size. You tell him that you bought the large vase from a friend who was selling everything she would not be able to fit into a smaller house in another town. She was a poet who had to move because she lost her job at the university.

You come back into the living room with the roses, but there is nowhere to put them. On every surface there are piles of books and papers.

He asks you how long you have lived here, and you're not sure if he means in this city or in this apartment. He might be trying to give you the benefit of the doubt. He might think you've just moved in and that's why the living room is still a mess. Or that you've just moved to this city and that's why you've answered his ad in the personal column.

"Four years in July," you tell him.

You smile. He smiles.

He describes the town he lives in, the state capital, which, he insists, is not as dull as everybody says it is. "There are some interesting shops," he says. He loves antiques.

"Do you enjoy going to flea markets?" he asks.

No, you do not, you say. You already live in one. Complete with fleas.

He knows you are joking, but he shifts in his chair, looks uneasy. The very idea of fleas seems to make him want to itch.

It is time to decide on a restaurant. You suggest one. He asks about another. The one he has mentioned is too expensive. The one you have in mind has good food at reasonable prices, and, what's more, you'll be able to talk.

That's why he has come. To talk. To get to know you.

You are in his car, which is large, you remark, and he says, yes, it's old, but it has served him well. "Ah," you say, "but it must eat a lot of gas." And he says, "No, not really as much as you'd think." Besides, he continues, he feels safer on the highway driving a big American car. "Those little foreign models fold right up around you in a serious accident." You nod, staring straight ahead, as he starts the engine. You hope he has not had many serious accidents.

The restaurant is crowded. Couples are seated at tables to the right and left of yours. You sit on a bench against a half-wall that separates the bar from the restaurant. Stanley sits facing you, grinning. You smile and look down at the menu. He asks what you recommend. You tell him that the vegetable pie is very good. He says he feels like roast beef. He asks you if you are a vegetarian. You admit to being carnivorous.

He smiles. You smile.

When the waitress comes, he orders a gin and tonic. He asks for a kind of gin you don't recognize. "It's English," he explains. They do not have that sort of gin, so he orders another. You have a Molson. It's Canadian, but you don't bother to mention this; he probably already knows.

He is talking about restaurants in his town. There is one he says you would like. "Bohemian" is the word he uses to describe it. You try to remember the last time the word "bohemian" came up in a conversation. You try to remember a time when the word meant something to you. Twenty years ago, maybe. And yet he thinks of you in this way.

He is talking about his stereo system, his collection of classical records. King's College Choir. Pachelbel's Canon. Several operas. "Do you like opera?" he asks hopefully. No, you are afraid you do not much, but, you are quick to add, you are not familiar with very many, and so it's probably a good thing they're performing more of them in English. Stanley does not agree. He is very nice about it, but there is nothing, he says, like Puccini in Italian, Wagner in German; no, nothing like the original.

The waitress clears the plates. You order coffee. You ask Stanley how long the drive is back to the state capital. An hour and a half, he says, then orders another gin and tonic, his fourth. You're almost sure this means he will be staying over, and you have decided you do not want him to.

All evening you have been looking for something to dislike about him, which is hard, of course, because he is so nice. He has brought you roses. He has let you choose the restaurant. He has said he liked the food, and that you made a good choice. He has been attentive. He has not put up a big stink because you do not like opera. He has not humiliated you in public.

He is talking about what he did before becoming a comptroller. He describes a time when he was concerned about causes and tells you about his troubles in graduate school, when he was studying political science and economics. He describes a seminar paper he wrote about a minor revolutionary figure in South America who, he insists, was every bit as important as Ché Guevara. The professor did not agree, and did not like Stanley, so he gave the paper a *D*. After that, Stanley says, he left graduate school. He looks dejected, and you feel sorry for him. You wish he'd stayed in graduate school. You like to think he might have become something more interesting than a comptroller. He knocks back the last of his gin and tonic and orders another. "Every revolution," he says, "eats its own children."

He is getting aggressive. He is raising his voice. He speaks emphatically, as though he cares about what he is saying, but it has a false ring to it. He is making a speech, trying to impress you, and you are relieved to have found this to dislike about him, relieved to have found something to balance against his good manners, the compliments he has paid you, the roses.

It's getting late. He has had too much to drink. He will probably have to spend the night with you. You wonder what it will be like, sleeping with him. You wish you had time alone to think about it. You wish you didn't have to find out this way.

How has it come up? How has he hit upon the subject of slavery? You've been wondering what it would be like to sleep with him, and now he is saying with perfect assurance, quite matter-of-factly, "Of course, there is nothing inherently immoral about slavery."

You cannot have heard him right, so you ask him to repeat what he's just said. You say you are sorry; you weren't listening. He says it again, and you're stunned. You disagree. You bring up the Civil War, the Emancipation Proclamation. You explain that your ancestors all fought in the Union Army. His did too, he says, but he's not bound by their decisions. He grins, a loose and crooked sort of grin. The Greeks, the Romans, he insists, treated their slaves very well; there were laws to protect them, and slaveholders in the American South often treated their slaves kindly without any laws at all. In fact, many slaves were better off under their masters than they were after they were freed.

"That's not the point," you say. "No one should have the power to own another human being." You want to jump up and sock him in the jaw, overturn the table, storm out of the restaurant. You feel as though he has just kicked you in the stomach and you must force yourself to keep breathing. But making scenes will never do. Lunging for his throat, clawing his eyes out will never do. It's that he sounds so smug, so reasonable. It strikes you suddenly that he is enjoying this. You have this horrible thought: that he thinks you're cute when you're mad, that your anger excites him, that he might be getting an erection.

He sits back in his chair, head cocked, smiling, triumphant. Anything you say now will only get you in further. You signal the waitress for the check. You pay for your meal. He pays for his. You divide the tip evenly, and then leave.

Why will you tell him, once he is inside your door again, that he should feel free to stay, that you can't have him driving all the way back to the state capital at this hour? He already expects it, and you wonder at what point you gave it away, at what point he decided he had the right to assume.

He is brushing his teeth in your bathroom, gargling a little garbled tune. You smoke one last cigarette in the living room before bed. You wonder why it costs so much, why it seems to cost so much to meet a man, to date, to start sleeping with him. You wonder if you will ever be like others who seem to manage this sort of thing quite easily. You're afraid you've botched it. You feel you have something to prove to yourself: that you can do it, that you can remain civil to this man who is gargling and humming in your bathroom, that you can sleep quite casually with someone you are beginning to despise.

When you walk into the bedroom, you discover he is the sort of man who tucks his T-shirt into his Jockey briefs. He is diligent in his hygiene, particular about his person. He lines his shoes up next to the bed, folds his trousers, folds his shirt, and places them neatly on a chair.

In the morning he leaves without the breakfast you offer to fix him. He dresses quickly, averting his glance from yours. He looks tired, hung over. Neither of you has slept well, not that the sex was extraordinary. It was sufficient. It got done. It's that neither you nor he is used to sleeping with anyone else, much less each other.

You stand inside your front door. Stanley is ready to leave. He promises to call. You know he won't, but say you hope he will. You think: let's not repeat this.

You smile. He smiles.

The roses are recriminations. Their twelve heads loll, motionless in the stale air. They have peach flesh tongues with scarlet edges. You wish they had come from someone you cared about. They are the first roses anyone has ever brought you, and they have come from the wrong man. They mock you for imagining you could slip with anything like grace, with anything like ease into the sort of life others seem to lead . . . this business of seeing someone.

Voici! Henri!

*N*ow I've done it. I've tossed Henri's things right out the window. The meaning of this will surely not escape Madame DuClos. Christ! The street is strewn with expensive shirts, designer jeans, his precious black bikini briefs.

There's someone at the door downstairs. It might be him. I'll just go and have a look . . . Blast! Damnation! It's Madame. I don't dare lean out the window and say, "Good evening, Madame, I thought you might be Henri," because she'd ask where he was; she'd say she hadn't seen him in weeks—ever since he left on holiday to . . . it was Switzerland, wasn't it? And then she'd laugh that deep down, hearty, malicious laugh she's got when she's having a really good time. She likes to see me suffer. Always has. I don't know why.

Oh she is poisonous, that woman: tiny, menacing, loud. And the pleasure she takes in my present circumstances is out-and-out sadistic. "Monsieur Henri seems to have found himself a new little friend," she says, "and a huge and beautiful car with a chauffeur," she says. "How does it happen that you never go with the young monsieur and his new friend, who is foreign, *n'est-ce pas?*" She thinks she detects a bit of a German or Austrian accent. "Perhaps he is Swiss," she says.

"He is," I say, "a business associate of Monsieur Henri."

"Oh?" she says, and here she raises one eyebrow—I've always envied people who can do that, it's the pinnacle of scorn. "*Comme les autres,* like the others?" she asks.

Ah, she is vicious, *absolument vicieuse.* You see she seems to believe I'm Henri's pimp or something, though she always refers to me as the *intellectuel.* The man of letters, she calls me. She herself is a worker, she describes herself that way, so when we first moved in, as a Marxist, I naturally tried to engage her sympathies, but she would have none of it.

"It's all very well for foreign intellectuals," she says, "but there's nothing in Marx for the workers. I remember the days of *le Front Populaire* and the sit-down strikes. I marched. I sang. It was all very exciting, but they didn't beat the Germans, they didn't stop *les boches,* did they? No! It took the Americans and General Charles de Gaulle to do that! And now. See what we have today. Look at my France, *ma pauvre France:* overrun with foreigners," and she narrows her gaze right at me.

She's out there now, shouting up, "Monsieur Edmond! What are all of these clothes doing in the street?"

I don't see why she assumes they came from our apartment. I mean, we're not the only ones living here. They might have come flying out of any number of other windows.

"*Je sais, Madame,* I know. A little mishap. Cleaning. I got a little overzealous. I'll be right down to fetch them."

"I should hope so," she yells. "I should hope so."

I didn't toss the photograph. I couldn't bear to. It's the one in the Pierre Cardin frame with the mauve mat which sets off Henri's black hair so beautifully. It's not bad of me either.

Voici! Henri! L'homme que j'adore.

The serious student of French will, no doubt, take note of the construction, the man I adore. He might well ask why it is not the other way round, *l'homme qui m'adore,* the man who loves me.

But one is never adored by the one one adores. Not ever in the same moment. I think it runs counter to the physical laws of the universe. Though he is, Henri is, really quite fond of me. At least he says he is, usually, or he did, usually, until he went on holiday last summer to one of those fishing villages along the Costa Brava and met—the Baron von.

Henri ne restera pas longtemps chez moi. Henri is not long for this household, I think. Though I'd never chuck him out. Oh no. Not when you're my age, you don't. You wait till he leaves on his own, then you give others to believe it was your idea, but you never say that outright. People would come away thinking . . . something you'd rather they not. At least I wouldn't want them to, you know, think what they usually think—the worst. And there are worse ways, I suppose, for *cher Henri* to take his leave from me than on the arm—though it will most likely be in the backseat of the chauffeur-driven Mercedes—of the Baron von.

Henri is really quite bright. Though he is busy living the un-examined life and has not the sort of intellect that is drawn to books, he is very shrewd. Oh yes, he is. He has what the French call *intelligence du coeur,* which is intelligence of the heart, which is something the French say about the Italians, which is sort of a gentle way of saying they are stupid, which they are not, of course, and neither is Henri. I don't mean it in that sense. I mean he is so generous, one is just naturally inclined to trust him. I love that about Henri. I do. He has this sense about people when they are needing attention, and he gives it to them freely, and often it's just the thing that's wanted. One can tell by their faces, the way they open to receive him.

He has, in addition to this *intelligence du coeur,* he has what you might call *intelligence de la poche,* intelligence of the pocket-book. He has this knack of finding people with enough money to take care of whatever it is he is wanting just then. He's always in the right place at the right time, ready to receive small and not-so-small favors. But that makes him sound like a terrible con, *un mauvais type,* which he is not at all. He's quite the sweetest boy you'd ever want to know. Well, boy, he's twenty-eight, but he's a young twenty-eight, if you know what I mean. Quite lively. Very inventive. Henri is always spontaneous, a real *bon vivant. Comme on rigole quand Henri est là.* The trouble is, he's not often *là.* Not here, that is, not present, so it's difficult to laugh as much, *c'est tellement difficile* to *rigoler,* because these days he is usually off with the Baron von, who is not actually a baron but a baronet, a fact which I would point out to Henri, did it not seem so petty, for it's not the title he's after so much as the . . . well, you see the Baron has quite a bit of money, and Henri has always liked nice things, and it takes me a long time to earn the money to buy them for him. Sometimes I do four translations in a month, arduous ones, from Russian to German to French and then into English— enough to make your head swim, and mine often does, but oh! the pleasure on that beautiful face when I walk through the front door with a cashmere sweater, gold cuff links, or something delicious to eat like truffles. But with me, he has to wait. Translations take time. Not everyone is always wanting them done. And with the Baron . . .

Though you mustn't get the wrong idea. Henri works too. When he can find it. In restaurants mostly. To watch him is to see the mere act of waiting tables elevated to High Art. And I'm not joking. He has a certain genius for it. It helps, of course, that he is very handsome, but that's only part of it. He is able to make ugly women feel ravishing and old men feel alive all over.

He models occasionally for one of the men's fashion maga-zines. And there was that *film,* though it was not a film; it was pornography without any pretense to art at all. We argued about it bitterly.

"It's just money," he said.

"No," I said, "when people are forced to degrade themselves and others to get it, it is not just money but something pernicious."

"What is degrading?" he cried.

And I could never explain it to him, so then he'd change tactics and call me a Communist, *un euro-communiste,* because I am ambivalent about money, I always have been, and so I would quote the head of the French Communist party at him, you know, "A Communist can be a good Catholic, there's nothing at all contradictory about that"—Henri despises the Church almost as much as he despises Marchais and the Communists—and he would say, "Balls!" or the French equivalent, and I would laugh then because he is such a *petit bourgeois,* Henri is, and he's the one who sprang from the loins of the proletariat. Not I. Oh my no. I'm as upper middle class as they come, which is why I'm a Marxist and he is not, you see, for I know the upper middle class for what it is, and Henri only knows it for what it likes to appear to be, and so he is quite conservative, politically. Every bit as bad as Madame DuClos. I'm surrounded by Gaullists and Vichy sympathizers! Why, if General Pétain were alive today, he'd have Henri's unequivocal support—or worse, his complete devotion. Well, what do you expect? He doesn't read. He merely parrots what he hears from the men who buy him drinks in the bistros. What I can't fathom is why they seem to talk nothing but politics in bed.

Yes. He goes to bed with them, and if they are rich Henri is the one who brings home the truffles and a bottle of Château Neuf du Pape. What can I do? I don't like it, but I can't exactly tie him to the bedpost—of course I could, one does, one often hears about it, but it's not the sort of thing that appeals to either of us. So there is nothing to be done. It makes me jealous. He says they mean nothing to him. He always says that, but it gives me a curious feeling, that they mean nothing to him, and I do, and his going off with them makes me suffer, and yet he does it, though they mean nothing to him, and why would anyone go and do something that meant nothing to him, go and do it again and again? Of course the extra money is quite nice, but we do not, we have not ever seen this in the same way.

It has to do with understanding how delicate, how temporary life is and how in the flick of a wrist it can be snatched away, or it can drain off a little at a time as you stand by and watch, helpless to do anything. Perhaps one has to have come nose to nose with death, one's own, the possibility of one's own, or someone else's. But even then, we all know people who do not see it. I mean surely, once one has had that experience, once one sees life turn from one and start away, one can never say it has no meaning.

What, then, can it mean? That he is not here?

Oh! I long for the old days when we were first getting to know one another and I knew where he was. I like to think of those days, they give me solace, often they do, but sometimes they do not; they make me feel old and unwanted, used up—cast aside. And for what! For whom! A baronet posing as a baron and simply because he has the money to buy *cher Henri* whatever his little black heart desires. It's the humiliation I can't bear. I've had him— you know, had him around—for eight years. I must be scared to death of losing him. Just look at me. I've broken out all in a sweat. What will I do without him? How shall I live? I've grown so used to him, and now—how can I make room for this grief? For it will take up room, more room than I have here in this apartment that's become so full of associations of *cher Henri*. Or maybe the grief will fill up the space he has left, fill it up nicely, oh yes, and grow, feeding on the furniture, sucking all the oxygen from the rooms, until it heaves, rising up larger and larger to choke me.

Or I could move—far, far away from Madame DuClos—take a smaller flat, sort of squeeze the grief out of my life, but then the grief might fill it up when I'm not looking, might crowd me out of my own home, and I'd have to take all my meals in cafés and go for long walks to keep myself busy, for there'd be no room in my flat for me. Every cubic centimeter of it would be filled with his absence . . . and my own sense of failure.

But wait. He hasn't left yet. There I go jumping to conclusions, when he's not actually left me. Not yet. I must remember that. Yes. That steadies me. He hasn't even mentioned leaving me. Of course he isn't leaving me! How could he? I am his life as much as he is mine. Except that's not quite true. I'm the one who's in danger, not Henri. Never Henri. Even so, I must keep things in perspective. He has not yet announced that he's going off to the Isle of Capri with the baronet—odious little man, he always smokes cigars, with his scarlet cummerbund stretched too tight over his belly full of the world.

Madame DuClos seems to be quite taken with the Baron, despite his German accent. When push comes to shove, she'll go for the title, no matter what its country of origin. She feels that democracy went terribly wrong somewhere along the line and the only thing left to save us is the restoration of the monarchy. "After all," she says, "it's just like what we've got now with this bureaucrat above the next, all the way up to the *président de la république,* but with kings, it's more amusing, we have more interesting people to talk about, as you have in England, Monsieur Edmond"—and she looks at me, as though she were thinking there might be hope for me if only I liked Queen Elizabeth.

So I think she encourages Henri and his friendship with the Baron. And she flirts with the Baron. She does. I've seen her. She'll notice his car waiting in the street below, and then she runs to put on a dress and one of her old turbans and some rouge, *et voilà*! There she is, hanging out of her window, screeching, "*Bonjour, Monsieur Henri, Monsieur le Baron,* you have such a lovely day for your outing"—that's what she calls them. And anyone can see she's just aching to have a ride in the Mercedes. Anyone, that is, except the Baron, who never offers. He's far too obtuse. Besides, he wants to get Henri away as fast as possible because there I am in another upstairs window, sometimes leaning out to wave, and at others, peering through the partly opened shutters.

I make him a little nervous. I like making him a little nervous, just to remind him that I'm still in the picture. So I wave. *"Bonjour, Monsieur le Baron. Amusez-vous bien."* Then I ask when they are getting back, or I shout out a time when I'd like Henri to return, and Henri rolls his eyes up at me, the Baron says nothing, and off they go, waving at Madame before they disappear behind the tinted windows—I wonder if they're bulletproof— and Madame waves and shouts after them and then asks me again why it is I never happen to go with them, and then she smiles that awful smile.

But he hasn't left me yet, Madame. The gold-plated razor that was my Christmas gift to him last year still sits on the ledge above the bathroom sink. I wonder how he shaves when he's away.

So we are still together, Henri and I, the only difference being he is never here. This time he's been gone for weeks. I don't know what to think. "Think what you want," he would say. *"Pense ce que tu veut, ça m'est égal,* it's all the same." He might well say that. Isn't it funny, when a lover's gone for a time, and not always a long time either, one forgets what he would say, one almost forgets what he looks like, so one consults the photograph, or one is brought back suddenly to the image of his face by the smell of his shampoo on the pillow. "Oh yes," you say. "I remember, yes, he used to live here, he used to lie right there beside me, and if I close my eyes and concentrate, yes, there is his smile, that particular one, sly, teasing, the one I loved best."

Of course, one cannot hold onto people. It never works. And I suppose I always knew Henri would be, as it were, buggering off one day. Though I ought not to be so callous. I'm quite sure he has some genuine feeling for the Baron, though I personally cannot see why. The man has not made much of an impression on me. Still, it's that Henri has not yet removed his personal effects—the ones I tossed out the window—that gives me reason to believe that this thing, this affair of the heart, this whatever it is with the Baron that is supposed to mean nothing actually does. Mean nothing. I mean that it will come to nothing, and Henri will once again come home to me, though he has not actually left.

If he were coming in tonight, I'd know how much supper to cook. If it's just me, I won't bother. I'm not eating much these days, but if Henri were to walk through the door and he hadn't eaten—why, I can't even think what I've got in the larder. Tinned meats mostly, for emergencies. But if I went out to buy food, I might miss him. He might telephone and, finding me not here, assume I'd gone out, which I would've done, but I'd have been right back and he'd have no way of knowing that. And if I did go out to do the marketing for the both of us, and Henri didn't come home, I'd have endives rotting in the fridge, apples moldering in the bowls, onions decaying in the baskets that hang from the kitchen ceiling.

It's the waiting I hate, the uncertainty. Oh Sweet Mystery of Life at Last I've Found Thee, but I wish you'd call to let me know you're going to be late, telephone or leave me a note when you're planning to stay away. And yet I dread the note that will read "Cher Edmond—I've gone off with the Baron forever. Please send my things. *Je t'embrasse. Grosses bisses! Henri.*"

If I still had friends, they'd say I was a fool. They'd tell me to get on with my life. They'd insist that I have it out with Henri and force him to make a choice. But they couldn't know, for I'd never be able to tell them, how frightened I am he'll make the wrong one. Leaving me is always the wrong choice, though the ones who leave never seem to come round to that idea themselves. Off they go, and all I can ever hope is that they'll regret it some day, and yet not one has ever come back to tell me that it ruined his life. In fact, one actually had the temerity to approach me at the theatre when I saw him again after we had parted ways, and he said leaving me was the best thing he'd ever done for himself, and then he thanked me, he embraced me and thanked me, and I just stood there in the foyer of the Comedie Française: stunned, dumbfounded—aghast. I couldn't think of anything to say. So I took Henri by the arm and led him away without introducing him.

Christ! There she is again, caterwauling in the street. All right. All right. "*Ça va, Madame. Je viens tout de suite.*"

She adores Henri. It's me she can't stand. And so she is always spying on us and always a little too polite to me and always giving me veiled threats about Immigration and the authorities: have I remembered to register with the police again this year? "You know they are getting very strict," she says. "*À cause des arabes,*" she says—all of whom she believes to be terrorists. So we are rather cagey around one another, she and I.

But what am I to say? How shall I explain the clothes in the street? Well, Madame, Henri is sweet, he's quite the lovely little morsel, and as he is French he loves the finest things money can buy, and well, it's evident, isn't it, that the Baron's got money, and you can see for yourself, *regardes moi,* that Henri's tastes run to older men. Yet you must remember, *ma chère Madame,* we have, Henri and I, something very special between us. The Baron means nothing to him; Henri says so himself. No, Madame, between me and the *jeune Henri* there is a history, eight years together, an unbreakable bond. Why, I practically raised the boy, Madame, I helped to create him, he could never turn his back on that, now, could he? He will be back, I know Henri, he'll come home, and you'll see, we will be happy again, singing, shaking the rugs out the window, tumbling out of a taxi, home from the bars, drunk and laughing and trying not to wake you, Madame. Surely you understand love. Surely you had in your youth the attentions of some young man, your husband perhaps. And surely you know, Madame, what it is to be no longer young, and how often one's greatest fear is of growing old alone. I don't mean to give offense, Madame, I'm sure you make out quite well on your own, but you see it's something I'd like to avoid myself, so as you may have noticed, I am rather distraught with Henri running off everywhere with the Baron von Deutschemark, the Baron von Mercedes, the Baron von house on Capri. And if this is it, if this is the night he fails to return, if this is the night which marks the onset of a life without love, I doubt, Madame, I shall ever be able to look you straight in the eye again.

Rita and Maxine

*R*ita Foelker sat at her table, staring at the narcissus bulbs she had tried to force. She'd been waiting for weeks for them to bloom. The leaves had risen out of the bulbs about a foot and a half, but the stalks had grown only four inches, and the little bloom pods had turned brown and were bending over as if they'd been lynched. When she got the bulbs, someone had told her to put a teaspoon of vinegar into the water so the leaves and stems wouldn't grow too tall and fall over the way they did each year. Rita had evidently put too much vinegar in the water, and instead of simply dwarfing the narcissus, she had killed the blooms outright.

"Look at it this way," a friend had said. "You've still got something green in your apartment. That should be enough." But it wasn't. The whole point of forcing narcissus in January was to have live flowers to look at, and here she had gone and poisoned them. So she sat, glaring at them, with her jaw set and her hands opening and closing into fists, first one and then the other.

Pursing her lips, she ran her tongue over the tooth she had chipped three days earlier. She'd been eating a piece of pizza, and the corner of a lower front tooth had fallen off. It made her feel old and brittle, as though anything could give way now. Her back ached. Her knees ached. She was underweight. Her heart might pop before she hit her fortieth birthday. It'd serve them right too—her producer, the board of directors, the goddamned subscribers.

Rita laughed as she unwound the gold plastic band to open another pack of cigarettes, her third today, or her second, if she were counting from midnight to midnight. Or her first, if she were counting from going to bed and getting up again, which she'd already done once that night, though she hadn't slept. It suddenly struck Rita as absurd that she was sitting up at four in the morning, staring down her narcissus and worrying about a chipped tooth, as though she had nothing else on her mind. Which was not true.

She was in trouble, deep trouble. The last play she had directed had not been a success. In fact, the last two years' worth of plays she had directed had not been successes. That's how the hottest "new" director on the contemporary scene of five years ago had ended up in St. Louis. She'd taken the scenic route from New York, via San Francisco and Minneapolis. And now she was in St. Louis, trying to save her ass with a revival of Ibsen. Which was safe. Nobody could object to Ibsen. Unfortunately, no one in the cast she'd hired, whose credits were nothing but soap operas and summer stock, could *act* Ibsen, and if this play failed . . . But she couldn't think about what she'd do if this play failed. It was too dangerous. The actress she had cast as Nora was the one bright spot. Maxine MacCaffrey had made a name for herself on both sides of the Atlantic, and her work had always impressed Rita. She was versatile, an actress of the old school—dignified, professional, a bit remote. Rita had auditioned her in New York, and she was beginning to hope MacCaffrey might even save this production. Rita's real worry now was that MacCaffrey would act circles around the other members of the cast. And she was a little afraid of Maxine. It had been quite some time since Rita had directed an actress who knew what she was doing.

Rita went to the small refrigerator, which the hotel staff kept calling an "ice box," and took out a plate with a leftover pork chop on it. She unwrapped the plastic and set the plate on the table. Then she turned back to the refrigerator and crouched down to look for the dish of garlic mayonnaise she'd made to go with the pork chops. She thought about sticking the pork chop into the toaster oven, but she was too hungry. Once she found the garlic mayonnaise, she poured herself a small tumbler of brandy and sat down to eat, chewing carefully to avoid her chipped tooth. She'd have thrown away the narcissus bulbs, but she wanted to wait a few more days just in case there were new stalks—any possibility at all of a bloom.

If this play failed, Rita would probably go to Europe and make a film. She'd had a letter some weeks earlier from a friend in Berlin who wanted to make a film about West German political prisoners held for long periods of time in solitary confinement. It was, her friend said, a brutal kind of psychological torture. Her first thought had been to make a documentary, but the authorities had denied her access to prisoners, so she was at work on a script based on interviews of women who'd been acquitted and later released. Rita could not stop thinking about those women and the small cells they were locked in. She thought about camera angles. She imagined close-ups of the women's faces and how she'd light them.

When she was in high school, Rita had been the only girl on the lighting and sound crew. That's how she got her start in the theater. She'd been too tall and her face too broken out to be an actress. Later, she became the assistant director because she liked being close to the source of power, in this case Mr. Harris the drama teacher, and she found that she liked telling people what to do. She learned a lot from Mr. Harris.

One night after a long rehearsal, they stayed behind together in the auditorium to go over some of the blocking. Out of the blue, he stuck his hand down Rita's jeans, which were loose-fitting because even then she'd been underweight. Mr. Harris had a reputation for feeling up the pretty girls who usually sang the lead in *Brigadoon* or *The Mikado,* but Rita figured she was safe because she was so ugly. Besides, she had always thought Mr. Harris really preferred boys, so she was surprised when she felt his hand squirming around in her pants. So surprised that she shoved him away, drew her right arm back, and hit him in the face. She felt something give way under her fist and hoped it was the bridge of his glasses, not his nose, but she didn't stick around to find out. She grabbed her coat and ran for it.

When she calmed down later at home, she thought she had ruined her chances for—everything; she wouldn't be allowed to continue as assistant director, she'd get expelled from school, she wouldn't be able to go to college. But the next day at rehearsal, Mr. Harris explained that he'd run into a door and broken his nose, which everybody believed because he drank a lot. Then he turned to Rita, smiled, and they got on with their work.

She had, by this time, eaten all of the pork chop she was going to eat. She thought about her dental appointment in five hours and the script read-through scheduled at the theater after that. Rita decided she ought to at least try to get some sleep, so she poured the rest of her brandy into the bowl of gravel that held the narcissus bulbs and went back to bed.

Maxine MacCaffrey threw off the covers and sat up in the middle of her bed. She was shaking. She'd awakened from a nightmare. She had handed her lover a supper plate. She had served him peas, potatoes, and a large steak. He had handed the plate back to her without a word. When she looked down at it, the steak was teeming with maggots. In the dream, she'd thought nothing of it. She'd taken the plate back to the kitchen, picked up the steak, and run it under the faucet, but the maggots had begun worming their way up her fingers and into the flesh of her hand and arm, so she'd dropped the steak into the sink and started to scream. That's what she was doing when she woke up. It was a quarter to five in the morning.

She pulled the cover over her legs and turned on the small lamp on her bedside table. Then she reviewed the objects in her room: pocketbook, room key, the script on the desk, and next to it, a neat pile of letters from England, all unopened. She knew what they said. "Dearest Maxine. Come back. I can't live without you." She could no longer think of his happiness as something which depended upon her. She could not spend her life smoothing his forehead and drawing his bath and planning dinner parties that were designed to win back actors and production staff who were threatening to quit. So she left London. She came home, though she'd never been to St. Louis. She came home to America.

But America didn't feel like home to her yet. The accent grated on her, and people gave her funny looks when she spoke. When someone asked her how she was, she said, "Very well, thanks." She said, "Sorry" when she needed to get past someone at the supermarket, and more often than not, the person would answer, "What for? You didn't do anything wrong."

She had forgotten how to use an American pay telephone. The money felt strange to her, too light and tinny; all the bills were the same size and color. She had forgotten which way to look before crossing a street.

People called it jet lag. People called it culture shock. But Maxine knew that the foundation of her psyche had been jarred, leaving everything that rested on top slightly askew and precariously balanced.

What Maxine wanted now almost more than anything else in the world was a room with whitewashed walls, a narrow bed, a writing table, clean surfaces, a window that looked out onto a courtyard, and, beyond that, a field, a view of the mountains. She would rise at dawn, wash her face, arms, and breasts in a basin of cold water. She'd dress quickly in a black frock and tie her hair back in a knot. It was a room she could live in without wigs or makeup. Stripped bare, a whole room stripped bare, with herself in it as herself, silent and still. But then that would be a way of playing the nun. She almost did not know how to stop acting.

Even now, as she sat up in bed with her arms wrapped around her legs, she saw herself playing the role of a distraught woman, an actress waking from a nightmare, a woman who has left her lover in another country.

She got out of bed, crossed the room, and picked up the script that was lying on the desk. She lit a cigarette and started turning pages. She was too tired to play Nora; she'd have much rather auditioned for Mrs. Linde, the one whose husband is already dead and who says, "The last three years have been one long work day for me, Nora, without any rest. But now it's over." "What a relief for you," says Nora. But Mrs. Linde says, "No, not a relief. Just a great emptiness. Nobody to live for any more."

Rubbish, thought Maxine, as she tossed the script back onto the desk. It's all rubbish.

"When we get older," the dentist had said, "our teeth get brittle." Somehow that was the most offensive thing anybody had said to Rita in years, and she couldn't get it out of her mind as she fished in the pocket of her flight jacket for the keys to the theater. She did not want any part of herself to be getting brittle, and now she was feeling brittle all over—her nails, her hair, her feet. She'd come early so she could get some paperwork done before the actors arrived, but once she was in the lobby, Peter came lumbering up to her. He was over forty and still bounced, which irritated her. She'd have to do something about it. He fell into that category of actor Rita called "chorus boy"—tall, lithe, and pretty.

"How did you get in?" she asked.

"Gus is here. He let me in the stage door."

Peter said he had some questions for her . . . if she didn't mind, if she had a minute. She did mind, and she didn't have a minute, so she told him to wait until after the read-through. She knew what kind of questions he had—mostly stupid ones. Peter was awfully sweet, but not very bright. He tried hard. She figured he was reading a lot about Norwegian life in the nineteenth century, trying to widen his frame of reference. He was one of those actors who'd done entirely too much television. He would need a lot of work, and Rita refused to deal with him just now, because if she started to think about the production, the whole thing would begin to unravel in her head.

She had no business, really, putting an actor like Peter on the same stage with Maxine MacCaffrey. He was too weak, and he'd be hard pressed to convince an audience he was Nora's husband and not the errand boy. The bounce would have to go. Rita cast plays these days the way she voted. She usually went with the one she hoped would do the least damage. Except for MacCaffrey.

Rita gave up the idea of paperwork. All she had really wanted to do was hide anyway, so she might as well hide in the theater. She walked in and took a seat in the middle of the fourth row from the back. She was tired. She didn't want to have to face Maxine MacCaffrey today. She was afraid that MacCaffrey might understand right off that this production was going to be second-rate, that Rita herself was . . .

Rita put on her sunglasses, leaned back, and closed her eyes.

Maxine felt the heel of her right boot hit the floorboards of the stage, and the sound seemed to resonate (or so she thought) throughout the theater. She was early. A little man with gray stubble on his chin had not wanted to let her in the stage door. She'd explained who she was and why she was there, but he said he had no instructions from Miss Foelker about any Maxine Mac-Caffrey. So she showed him a copy of her contract, which she'd brought along to give to Rita, and he let her in. But she could feel him watching her as she walked down the hall toward a large metal door with a note written in block letters on it that said: DON'T SHUT THIS DOOR TOO TIGHT OR YOU MIGHT NOT GET OUT. She turned to the little man, who'd said his name was Gus, and asked if this was the right door.

"Yes," he said, "but don't shut it too tight . . ."

"I know. I see the note," said Maxine. "Thanks for your help. You're very kind." And once she had walked through it, she slammed the door behind her.

The house was dark. She liked to be alone in a theater to get the feel of the place when it was empty. It was by no means the oldest theater she'd worked in, but it was old enough, worn enough to give her comfort. And already she could tell the sound carried as she listened to her wooden heel hit the wooden floor. She walked with long, slow, deliberate strides towards a folding chair, the only thing on stage. She focused all of her attention on that chair, grateful that it provided her with a direction to walk in, something tangible to reach. It was where she had to get to, and if she made it, she'd be all right. The simplest acts were what counted now. It didn't matter what country, which theater; she was onstage again.

Maxine folded her white wool coat over the back of the chair so it wouldn't get dirty. Then she picked up her script, turned, and walked to her left, reading to herself. She wanted to feel more for Nora than she did. She wanted to like Nora. It was an old disappointment. She was afraid the entire play was dated. Leaving one's husband and children these days was about as serious as having bad breath, so her job was to make Nora seem less trivial, less stupid than she'd seen her portrayed by other actresses, especially in Act One.

Maxine found herself back at the chair. She dropped the script onto the seat, locked her knees, and, bending over at the waist to stretch out the muscles in the backs of her thighs and calves, started to fish for a cigarette in her pocketbook.

"Miss MacCaffrey. As appetizing as your backside appears to be, it is customary to take a bow towards the audience, not away from it, and only after you've done something worthy of their applause."

Maxine froze. The voice was coming from the back of the theater, from somewhere beneath the first balcony. The voice belonged to Rita Foelker. Maxine could have stood up immediately, reeled around, and stood there mute, but she didn't. She stayed exactly where she was, found a cigarette, stood up slowly, lit it, dropped the lighter back into her pocketbook, turned to face the voice, and smiled.

"It is also customary, Miss Foelker, to announce oneself when one enters a theater, instead of sneaking up on people."

"For the next eight weeks, it's still my theater. I'll do exactly as I please. Besides, I was here first, MacCaffrey."

"Sorry. If I had known you were sitting there, I'd have greeted you properly."

"Properly indeed," said Rita, mimicking Maxine's faintly British accent. "Now. Put out your cigarette, put on your coat, and make your entrance again, only try not to look like you've just been to the morgue. Cross to the chair, take off your coat, take five steps upstage left, turn, and walk back to the chair."

Maxine put the cigarette out on the sole of her boot. She turned to her pocketbook, leaned over, bending her knees this time, and put what was left of the cigarette back into the packet. She rose, put her coat on, and walked offstage. She wanted to keep on walking, through the fire door she'd slammed earlier, down the hall, past Gus, and out of the stage door, but something in her insisted she walk back onstage and face Rita Foelker, so she turned and walked out from behind the scrim, her heels ringing against the floorboards, and stopped when she reached the chair.

Nora, dressed for outdoors, enters, humming cheerfully. She carries several packages, which she puts on the table, right. She leaves the door in the front hall open . . .

Maxine shrugged her coat off her shoulders and let it fall down her back till the collar reached her hand. She grabbed hold of the collar, lifted the coat, tossed it up, and caught it over her right arm—in one gesture. This was exactly what Maxine wanted for Nora. It showed a strong, precise, and almost deadly sense of purpose, and made it clear that Nora was in control, no matter how she made it appear to her husband, who called her his "little lark twittering," his "pouty squirrel." Nora is her husband's superior, thought Maxine. She certainly has more spine, more courage, at least morally, than he has. And she's got it from the start; that's what had to be clear.

"Good," said Rita. "That's good. Now. I want you to do an

improvisation. Let's say I've got this man sitting next to me. Let's say he's the handsomest, the most powerful . . . let's say he's got the biggest dick in St. Louis. Whatever you want; he's got it. He's a man with power over your life. You either manage to seduce him, or you're dead; he'll kill you. Got it? Now seduce him. No words. Just gesture. Whenever you're ready."

Maxine stood by the chair, staring out into the dark theater in the direction of Rita Foelker's voice, which sounded nearer to her than it had before. She was stunned a bit, and she was afraid Rita could read it on her face. And yet she knew she shouldn't be surprised. Rita had a reputation for this sort of thing. People made the mistake of thinking that just because Rita Foelker was a lesbian, she necessarily liked women. She did not. In fact, she did not appear to like anybody, and she was openhanded with her abuse; she let everyone have it. Maxine straightened her back, looked down, smoothed her skirt, and, as she noticed a new scuff on the outside of her left boot, she made a decision. If Rita Foelker went too far, she'd leave.

She stood for a moment like a penitent, with her hands folded over her skirt, face to the floor. She looked up and for a long moment stared into the blackness, as though she could not believe what she was being asked to do. Her expression was full of silent protest, the mouth a bit open, her brow drawn into a frown, as if she were shocked and expected her tormentor to be ashamed of himself. She relaxed her facial muscles in resignation, in surrender. She turned on her heel and took several slow steps toward the wings. She looked down at the stage, as if she were taking a moment to reconsider. Then, looking back into the dark theater, she smiled a shy deceptive smile which didn't reveal her teeth, and, as she did, she lowered her eyelids slowly. Just enough.

She turned again toward the wings and resumed her slow stride, then reeled around and stopped dead, facing Rita Foelker with her whole body. She looked off to her left, as though she were distracted by something, and then, smiling to herself, she began a slow dance in a big, loose circle, which tightened as she danced and turned, turned and angled her shoulders first this way, then that, quickening, now raising her arms as if she held a Spanish shawl and were whipping it around her head and letting it fly out in back of her as she ran, bounded, leaped, landed, pounded her boots on the floorboards, faster and faster, the circle growing smaller and tighter, until she stopped, crouched down, lifted her face, her breath coming in great short gulps, her shoulders heaving, and faced the empty stalls, sensing only then the chill that must have shot through Rita Foelker's body as she watched her.

Maxine now stood with her hands on her hips, feet planted wide apart. She threw her head back and started to laugh, a big, hearty, musical laugh that broke the tension and filled the theater. For a full minute, there was no sound after Maxine stopped laughing. She could almost hear the inside of Rita's head working, blocking scenes, rethinking Nora, questioning her choice of actor for Nora's husband. (He was too weak. Maxine would overwhelm him. Changing him would be easier perhaps than asking Maxine to hold back.) She moved her head around in slow rotations and moved her shoulders up and down to loosen the muscles. While dancing, she'd become a thousand women in rapid succession, all of whom had rallied and roused themselves in her, so that she would not have to stand up to this tyranny alone.

"Good," said Rita. "Very good. That was nice work." Her voice was quiet, and it now issued from a seat quite close to the stage. She had moved. Maxine nodded her head toward her.

"Now," said Rita, "I want you to tell me what you think of children."

Maxine thought for a moment and said, "Well, Nora loves her children, but she knows nothing really about being a mother to them. She treats them in the same way her husband treats her, and, as she says in the last act . . ."

"That's not the question, MacCaffrey. How do *you* feel about children? Have you ever had an abortion?"

Maxine did not look down or away. She smiled, the sort of perfunctory smile that never reaches the eyes, and said, "That's none of your business. I don't see what that's got to do with Nora."

"For the next eight weeks, *everything* is my business. You're going to have to cooperate. I don't give a shit about your personal life. But I do need to know if you've got the emotional resources to deliver the kind of Nora I want."

"Miss Foelker, my emotional resources are my concern, not yours. Now, if you'll excuse me . . ." Maxine turned to collect her coat and pocketbook and started walking toward the wings.

"Oh for Chrissake come back, MacCaffrey. Don't be so fucking sensitive. I'm *sorry*. All right?"

Maxine stood still for a moment, her back to Rita Foelker. She sensed that this was the closest Rita ever came to begging, not that she was interested in having her beg. It was the urgency in Rita's voice that arrested her. And now Maxine knew everything she needed to know.

It was Rita who broke the silence with a line from the play. "But dearest Nora—you look all done in. Have you been practicing too hard?"

Without hesitation, Maxine answered with her next line, "No, I haven't practiced at all."

"But you have to, you know."

Maxine turned toward the voice. "I know it, Torvald. I simply must. But I can't do a thing unless you help me. I have forgotten everything."

"Oh it will all come back. We'll work on it."

"Oh yes, please, Torvald. You just have to help me. Promise?

I am so nervous. That big party—. You musn't do anything else tonight. Not a bit of business. Don't even touch a pen. Will you promise, Torvald?"

"I promise. Tonight I'll be entirely at your service—you helpless little thing.—Just a moment, though. First I want to—"

Maxine turned to the wings and, trying to muffle the note of panic in her voice, said, "What are you doing out there?"

"Just looking to see if there's any mail."

"No, no! Don't Torvald!" cried Maxine.

"Why not?"

"Torvald, I beg you. There is no mail."

When Maxine turned to play the first bars of the tarantella on the piano that would be there once she was working with props, she stopped. Rita Foelker was standing in the wings, one hand in the pocket of a long woolen jacket with a frayed collar. In the other hand, she held a cigarette. She was watching Maxine with an intensity that startled her. Maxine looked at Rita, and for the first time saw, really saw, the legendary pockmarks left from the case of adolescent acne that had ravaged her face. Maxine was struck by how vulnerable she looked, how almost afraid she seemed, and she wanted to go over to Rita and take both her hands in her own. She wanted to reach up and touch Rita's face, with its hundreds of tiny open wounds, and tell her that everything was going to be all right, that she was safe, and that she had her wholehearted support and loyalty as an actress.

But before Maxine could take a step, Rita spoke one of Torvald's lines, "My dearest Nora, you're dancing as if it were a matter of life and death!" And Maxine answered, very quietly, "It is, Rita. It is."

"And so," said Rita, "we understand one another."

Bettina in Love

*The only woman awake is
the woman who has heard the flute!*
—Kabir

ll I am trying to say, Teenie hon, is that if you go on
like you are, you're liable to plié yourself right back into
St. Elizabeth's, and this time they might not get you
unfolded."

Bettina knew she should smile at Louise to show she was pay-
ing attention, but she was preoccupied. She wanted to tell Louise
about the crumpled-up coat she had found lying in the vestibule
of her apartment building, but this was not the time to bring it up.

"Bettina, are you listening to me? You look like you've floated
off into the ozone. Teenie! Come back."

Louise was waving her hand in front of Bettina's face.

"Yes," Bettina said in a hard, low voice, "I'm listening. You
were talking about Saint Elizabeth." Bettina looked around the
restaurant to see if anyone was watching. "And stop trying to
draw attention to yourself."

"Not Elizabeth the saint—St. Elizabeth's: the hospital. You

know, Our Lady of Thorazine? And what I am drawing attention to is the fact that you are working yourself to the very brink
of nervous prostration. Not only that, you are starving yourself.
Just look. You've barely touched your salad. Not eating properly and exhaustion lead to depression, and we both know where
depression leads you."

"Oh. Right," she said. "St. Elizabeth's."

"Bingo!" said Louise. "Now the point I am trying to make is . . ."

What troubled Bettina about the abandoned overcoat was that
it was still so cold outside, but it disturbed her even more that she
was afraid if she picked it up she'd find a shrunken woman, curled
in upon herself, growing tinier and tinier, until she was no bigger
than a pinprick.

". . . so if you're not careful, you're going to end up . . ."

"Just like my mother," said Bettina.

Louise stopped short. "That's not what I had in mind to say,
but now that you mention it, the idea bears some consideration.
Not that I have ever for a moment believed your condition was
hereditary. Or even that you had a condition. You know I've said
from the start, it's all in your head."

Bettina sat back and smiled, waiting to see how Louise was
going to talk her way out of this.

"You know what I mean. It starts with a bad attitude. Then it
gets in your glands and sort of leaches into your body, until you
are so depressed you cannot move a muscle, and, as you know,
this is a serious impediment to your dancing. Your mother's problem was she never fought my daddy, never once stuck up for
herself. She just lay down and took it."

"Every inch of it," said Bettina.

"About three times a week," said Louise.

She'd known Louise all her life. They'd grown up next door to each other, and even though they were the same age, Louise had always taken it upon herself to explain the world to her. It was Louise who'd sat her down one day when they were eleven and said, "Now listen, Teenie, I have to tell you something terrible. Your mother and my father are committing adultery." And when Bettina had failed to grasp what that meant, Louise rolled her eyes and explained the whole thing. "But how did you find out?" Bettina asked. "Never mind," said Louise, "the details are too horrible to recount," though she finally admitted she had walked in on them. "Caught them red-handed" is how she'd put it at the time.

And so they had lived for years with the secret that everybody in Baltimore must have known—through high school, through her mother's first breakdowns, through her subsequent hospitalizations and final suicide.

Now Bettina watched Louise scoop up a lump of manicotti she'd cut loose from one of the large bulbs of pasta lying in tomato sauce on her plate. Then she stared into her own small salad, lifted her fork, and put it down again. She was thinking about the abandoned coat in the doorway. She was trying to remember at what point her mother had begun to lose interest in living. "No matter what," she had always said to Bettina, "no matter how low you feel, you must always put on clothes, at least for a little while, every day." First they noticed she was sleeping later and later, and sitting up late into the night, roaming from room to room. And at first they all joked about it: her mother simply didn't keep the same hours as other people; she kept having to ask what day it was. But then, as she left her bedroom less and less frequently and forgot to dress even for a little while for days on end, they had learned to not speak of it at all.

"It's not as though I'm suggesting you give up the dance you're working on. Just go easier on yourself," said Louise. "Get out and have some fun. Go on a date. I don't recall reading anywhere that

Isadora Duncan ever denied herself a little pleasure."

"And look what happened to her," said Bettina.

"So go easy on the champagne, and stay out of Bugattis. The point is you'll never be happy, you won't even get this new dance staged if you don't plug your phone back in and leave off reading voodoo books."

Louise shook herself and made a face.

"*The Lives of the Saints* is not about voodoo," said Bettina, "and neither is *The Tibetan Book of the Dead.*"

"They might as well be for all the good they do. Don't you see? They're all about dead people, Teenie. It's morbid. You ought to get out and meet some people who are still alive. We're not so bad once you get to know us."

Bettina wanted to tell her about Michael, the man she'd chosen to dance the part of Krishna in this new piece she was making. She thought ahead to the kind of advice Louise might give her— advice she'd pretend to listen to and then ignore. Even so, Bettina had always listened when Louise sat her down and kept both hands on her shoulders so she couldn't fly away. For years she had listened awestruck to what she didn't want to hear: the mysteries of menstruation, what Billy Samuelson was really after, how to appear to be drinking and stay sober at college mixers. So this is it, she had thought again and again, the missing piece of information. But there had always been other pieces, secret bits of wisdom that eluded her, knowledge—it struck her now—that eluded them both.

Bettina watched Louise dip a piece of bread into the tomato sauce at the edge of her plate. She thought of all those Saturday evenings growing up: her parents and Louise's parents at the bridge table, drinking and arguing, and how the arguing and laughing got mixed up together, so it never seemed to make sense, shouting about points or a bad bid, then her mother running from the table in tears, and Louise's father comforting her in the kitchen, and all of them sitting down again to play another rubber.

Bettina wanted to remind Louise that Saint Teresa had once called life a "night spent at an uncomfortable inn." But Louise would get irritated. She had no patience with—anything. She was the irresistible force that had never met its immovable object. She had talked her way into and out of high school sororities, Marxist study groups, and two marriages. Then, in her second year of law school, her father died, leaving her quite a little bit of money, so she dropped out, got a perm, bought a condominium, and took up with a man named Chuck who wore string ties.

"This might come as a surprise," said Louise, "but I did not take you out to dinner to lecture you." She had her pocketbook in her lap and was looking deep into it. Then she pulled out a white envelope, set it on the table, and patted it once with her palm. "Your first check."

"Louise . . ." Bettina looked away and then down at the floor.

"Now quit, Teenie. We decided—well, I decided, but you did finally agree—that once my daddy's estate was settled, I'd share it with you. After everything he put your mother through, it's only . . ."

"Louise."

"All right. Besides, now that I'm a woman of the eighties—a retired revolutionary, not a shred of political consciousness left, with more money than she knows what to do with—I am going to invest in the future of American dance theater. I love you, hon. I want to help."

Bettina opened her mouth to say something and then shut it again. Her eyes had locked onto a point somewhere above and to the left of Louise's head. She could feel her face tighten.

Louise looked around to see what Bettina was staring at. A tall, broad-shouldered man with curly black hair walked towards them. He was followed by a small redheaded man who took quick military steps to keep up.

"Bettina," the taller man called out, "I thought that was you."

Louise turned and ran her gaze over Bettina's face to see what she could find out before the two arrived at the table. Bettina relaxed her jaw and tried to smile. She knew better than to look at Louise. She tried to think how to introduce Michael. A gifted dancer. The one I've chosen to dance the part of Krishna in my new piece. A man I'm afraid I'm falling in love with. And how to introduce Louise. My best friend. We grew up together. Her father used to screw my mother.

"I'm glad we ran into you," said Michael. "I wanted you to meet my friend Pat. He's a dancer in Los Angeles."

"I do television mostly," said Pat. He twisted up his face to indicate it was beneath him.

"I've been telling Pat about the work we're doing, and he says he'd like to see us rehearse. If that's OK."

"Why," said Bettina, "of course." But that's not what she meant. She wanted to leave it at "why." She meant "of course not." The work was too new, too raw, too strange to her. It wasn't ready for anybody to see yet. It was too private. She was appalled that Michael didn't know that.

His friend had a peculiar and very intricate haircut: short on the sides with tiny lines shaved close to the skull. His hair was longer at the back and curled behind his ears. On top, it stuck straight up with the help of some kind of tonic. Bettina knew it couldn't possibly be Vitalis, but for the life of her, that's all she could think of. In each ear he wore an assortment of small stones. And he had on entirely too much cologne.

"I'd appreciate it," he said. "Michael's told me so much about your work." He looked up at Michael, as if he were about to slip his arm around him. There was something proprietorial about the way he treated Michael, as if it were meant to signal something—something Bettina didn't want to acknowledge, something that shut her out.

"I'm Louise." Bettina had completely forgotten to introduce her. "And now that you mention it, I wouldn't mind seeing the work myself."

Michael's friend turned to Louise and offered her a sweet little grin that was meant to be irresistible. Louise was busy making him believe she found him utterly charming, though it was clear she didn't buy a bit of it. Shameless, thought Bettina. It was a word her mother would have used, and it fit Louise because Louise wasn't ashamed—of anything.

Then Louise turned to Michael. She simply warmed to him, opened herself in a way that asked nothing in return. Bettina could tell Louise liked him; she was enjoying herself. Louise asked them to pull up a couple of chairs and join them. Bettina lit a cigarette to cover up the redheaded man's cologne. Michael's friend said he was tired. Michael looked around the restaurant and said it would probably take a long time to get served. They were hungry. It was best to pick up something on their way home. "I'm only here for a few days," said Pat. "Michael and I don't have much time together."

Bettina coughed.

"See you tomorrow then," said Michael. And with that, he followed his friend through the tables and out of the restaurant.

When the two men had gone, Louise leaned over and put her hand in Bettina's. "So that's what's been eating at you," she said. "You're in love with him." Then she smiled and shook her head. "Of course you'd have a better chance if he were heterosexual." She leaned back. "Well, I'm going to have me some chocolate cheesecake. What are you going to have?"

Bettina thought of Michael. She thought of little else these days. He had the perfect stage presence—at once commanding and ethereal. She had auditioned scores of dancers for the lead, and she'd known right off that Michael was the one.

She sat at her desk, poring over diagrams of the dance she was trying to make. All around her were pictures of Krishna dancing with his flute, Krishna exalted in the heavens, Krishna revealing himself to the cowmaids, the subject of her ballet. She'd charted all the moves of Krishna's dances with the individual cowmaids and the ensembles. But she was troubled by his pas de deux with Radha, the one he chooses above all the others. Her part. She had it fixed in her mind, her moves and Michael's, but she couldn't work out the sequence, she couldn't get it down on paper. And she was afraid it would never come across—what it meant to Radha to be chosen by the Lord, what she sees and understands as she is overcome by Krishna.

She put out her cigarette and lit another. She stubbed that out as well when she looked at her watch and realized she'd be late for rehearsal and she had to stop by the post office before it closed.

She stepped into a long, black woolen skirt and pulled a white linen blouse over her leotard. She braided her hair and wound the braid around her head, shoving pins in to secure it. Michael had been amazed at its length. Down to her waist. She hadn't had it cut short since she was sixteen, the year her mother died. She grabbed a large, loose-fitting velvet hat from the top of her dresser and tightened the broad white band around her forehead. Joining one piece of cloth to another, she pierced both bits with a long straight pin, at the end of which was a bright red enameled star.

She went into the next room to fetch the package she'd wrapped earlier in the day. She was sending Michael a set of eight wine glasses. He'd mentioned the other day at the studio that he and Pat had bought a lovely bottle of wine but they'd had to drink it out of juice tumblers. She had wrapped each of the glasses carefully in a full page of want ads from the *Washington Post*. They were crystal. She'd bought them at the Wedding Shop. She wound strips of cotton in and around the newspaper bundles and tucked the rest down into the corners of the box and along the sides.

Even so, she was afraid the glasses might break. She could not help imagining it, and saw in her mind a shard of glass nose its way into the flesh of Michael's palm as he unwrapped the package. She saw him run his hand under the faucet, the water rinsing pink, then clear again, for it was only a superficial wound. It occurred to her that he might not be capable of sustaining any other kind, and she was surprised to find she could despise him for that. Then she pictured herself with his hand open on her lap as she picked the bloodied sliver of glass from his palm, saying, "Hold still. I'm only trying to help you."

"Stop it," she said out loud to herself. "Just cut it out." And yet she could not help how she felt. She could not stop thinking about his body. She was, after all, making this dance for him. And a great deal had come to rest on this ballet and what it meant. Of course, in the original story, it comes out all right: Radha ends up as Krishna's consort eventually. But Bettina's dance focused on the moment of revelation, and the delusion of each cowmaid when she believes Krishna is dancing only with her, embracing only her. It was Radha's own revelation that was the problem. It was the moment one stepped outside the normal realm of human love into another kind of reality. It was the experience of being reunited with God, and as such, the moment rested delicately on the edge of pure hokum. The trick was to let it be, not push it, let it hold its own integrity and truth.

She had it in her head all right, but how to make this ballet something other than a stage full of horny ladies gyrating around a beautiful man was something Bettina was beginning to fear was beyond her. She also knew she had come to a place in her life where she must dare to say this. Whatever it was she was trying to get across in this ballet, it wouldn't let her rest.

When she reached the vestibule, she shuddered, thinking of the abandoned overcoat. She pushed past the terror that came up in her again when she imagined what might be inside.

She slowed down. She had to steady herself, feel her feet on the pavement, remember to breathe. Louise said it never ceased to amaze her how unaware dancers were of their own bodies, as if they only used them to dance in and left them on a hook in the cloakroom the rest of the time. She breathed. She laughed out loud at Louise. She took large, confident steps along the sidewalk and whistled a phrase from Satie, a phrase from Mozart, fragments she could not connect because they jutted too fast through her mind.

She was sending a gift to Michael. He needed wine glasses. It was a friendly gesture. That's all there was to it. But she also knew he would think of her when they arrived. And she knew, secretly, in a small part of her heart, she was waiting for him to choose her.

She didn't like the looks of the man behind the post office counter. She'd been studying his face while she stood in line. He was short and squat and bald. His mustache did not quite hide the scar that pulled his lip into a nasty snarl. He was being unpleasant to an old woman at the moment. The woman leaned over with her good ear towards him and apologized a second time, and then a third; she didn't hear well. "Eighteen cents. I told you. You need eighteen more cents on this letter," he shouted.

Bettina's mother would have said something to reassure the old woman. She would have made a discreet comment about the clerk's bad manners, but because Bettina had a particular horror these days of ending up like her mother, she kept her thoughts to herself.

When it came her turn at the counter, she set the box down and took off first one, then the other lavender suede glove. She raised her head and gave the clerk a smile that shone with perfect contempt.

"Good afternoon," said Bettina. "I'd like to send this package first class." She put one hand on top of the box before the clerk could grab hold of it. "Gently," said Bettina. "It's fragile."

Bettina stopped to get her bearings. She'd been walking a long time through a neighborhood she didn't know. Michael's neighborhood. She kept telling herself this was innocent enough, she simply wanted to know more about him, and so she decided to follow them home from rehearsal, Michael and the young man from California who'd come to fetch him. She'd been careful to stay a few blocks behind them, stepping into an alley when she felt herself getting too close, running to catch up when they got too far ahead of her.

It was one of those neighborhoods people said was in transition, or, as Louise put it, "The poor we shall always have with us, they're just not going to live down the street anymore." A garage was being fashioned into shops and condominiums. Across the street, they were pulling down an apartment building to put up a garage. It reminded Bettina of a ceremony she'd read about to prepare a Tibetan monk for initiation and empowerment. Chanting, he fills a silver ring with rice, then places a smaller one on top, filling that, until he disassembles the structure and begins again, making and remaking the universe 100,000 times in order to perfect it.

In an alley, Bettina peered around a corner, waiting for Michael and his friend to move ahead, for they had stopped now under a street lamp for some reason—she could not allow herself to think they might be kissing—obscured by the trench coat Michael had taken off and held over their heads to protect them from the rain. Bettina pictured in her mind the entrance to the diamond path, that most sacred of mandalas, symbol of the Palace of the Gods. She thought about how one purifies oneself in readiness—molding the human heart, shaping, reshaping it. She feared that were she to pull her own heart open, it would reveal a monkey-faced woman pulling open her heart to reveal a monkey-faced woman pulling open her heart to reveal the same image of desire repeated endlessly inward.

She stood now in the shadow of a warehouse, wondering what it was to be changed into. It started to rain again, hard, so she moved along the wall and backed into a shallow doorway, without taking her eyes from the building Michael and his friend had run into across the street. She was waiting to see which window would suddenly light up. She scanned the floors, placing the apartments in her mind. It was a three-story building. Only one set of windows on the second floor was dark. She waited longer than she thought it should take them to light, surely longer than it would take the two men to get upstairs and in the door, unless they had left the lights on or Michael's apartment was in the back of the building.

Three squares of light appeared on the opposite wall; a large fern hung in the window to the left. Bettina flattened her back against the metal door to make sure she could not be seen. Michael's friend appeared in the window. He was looking out, and now Michael stood behind him with his arms around his waist. The redheaded man placed his hands over Michael's and looked up at him.

Bettina stared at them and at the yellow light that surrounded them in the window, as if she were studying a fresco in a church or an icon, trying to put it together, working to pull a story out of the image. She hugged her rain-soaked wool coat to her sides, but she could not draw it in tight enough to stop the question from rising in her—why him and not me?

She thought of crossing the street. She would ring the bell and wait for Michael to come open the door. She would explain that she'd been walking home—no—to the bus stop from a friend's house, and she'd seen him walk into his building, thought she'd stop by to say hello. He would invite her upstairs. Oh no, she didn't mean to intrude. Oh not at all, he would say. She'd sit and talk over tea. Of course, you're the man from California I met at the restaurant the other night. She would stay later and later and tire them out, so they wouldn't feel like making love after she left. But then she felt her body again, wrapped in wet wool and the heavy wet braid under the bright cloth she'd wound around her head: the lovelorn Radha of her ballet, waiting for Krishna while he dallied with another.

But she was no longer innocent. It was no longer a question of idle curiosity. She'd seen what she hoped she wouldn't see. She was a monkey spy, a malevolent spying ghost. She could not penetrate the spheres of diamond and flame, nor get past the magic dagger dieties who protected the Theater of the Gods. She could prevent nothing between Michael and the man now standing in his arms, as if he were enfolded in the wings of the archangel.

Bettina heard the sound of a car horn, one long blast and then another, and one by one dragons descended from the upper air. They lit the sky with flame. Vermilion touched the edge of cloud after cloud, and the clouds expanded and contracted too fast—too fast, as if the sky were churning with blood.

It was Thursday. They were rehearsing the new ballet in the dance studio. The glare from outside the window outlined Michael's head and sharpened the line of his shoulder. It seemed to move—did move—as he moved. It filled up the empty space as he turned and walked to the left.

What had first fixed Michael in her mind was the grayish-white glare that came from behind his head and torso, from under his arm as he lifted it, from under his chin, as he turned his head, as if he were holding the glare back to keep it from breaking the window and pouring into the studio to engulf them.

The glare from behind the studio window defined the shape of Michael's nose and cheek and brow. It seemed to lift him as he rose from his deep knee bends at the ballet bar, or as he raised one arm above his head.

At times Bettina thought the light emanated from his body. She was almost sure his body contained it, but that was not so. It could not be so, for the light was there even when he was not. Palpable. The glaring white light pushed in through the window, pulsing and beating. It shot a thin white line around one of his ribs and then another, and along the brass ballet bar, touching it with gold.

He rose. He descended. He turned and moved away into the light and back out of it again, towards her and away from her, as though she were not the only one dancing with him. She could see that the studio wall had disappeared and nothing separated them from the air five stories above the pavement. Still, he turned away into the light again, danced in midair, opened wide his arms, threw his head back, smiled, then stepped in toward her again.

It was as if the light, that hideous, grayish glare, the light had somehow—

Bettina stopped dancing. She put her hand to the bridge of her nose. "It's the light," she said. It had given her a headache. She could not continue. She needed a break. Did anyone have an aspirin, a cigarette? Couldn't something be found to cover the window while they rehearsed? Really, it was intolerable. "Doesn't it bother you, Michael? No? You don't find it distracting?"

It was what had first fixed Michael in her mind, that light. And then the knob of bone at the end of his shoulder. Then the shape of his rib cage, rising and pressing out against his flesh, changing the shape of his black leotard. And then his feet, carefully taped, a tiny clump of black hairs flattened by the tape on his big toe. It must hurt when he tears it off, she thought. How would she ever learn to do it so it didn't hurt him? So it didn't yank one precious hair from its follicle?

He was asking if she wanted to stop. But he was asking Louise, not her. Then Louise was at her elbow. "Do you want to stop?" Bettina looked at Louise. Did they think she was deaf? Light blinded; it didn't deafen. Then Bettina saw herself as though another woman's body were stepping out of her own, clad in a white tunic, her hair loosened from its braid. She watched this image of herself turn again towards Louise, reach up, and then fall into Louise's arms, howling. She sensed the presence of other women, several of the other cowmaids from some ancient village. Arms held her body. Hands smoothed her hair. She could hear their voices rise and fall, cooing, consoling her in her grief. And she watched herself thrash and weep.

But she was still standing. Louise was still at her elbow. Michael and the redheaded man from California stood by the window.

"No," said Bettina. "No, of course not. I just need a minute—five minutes. Can somebody give me a cigarette please? I'd like a drink of water."

"You want to know what I think?" whispered Louise.

"No. I do not want to know what you think right now, Louise. Just let me rest."

Bettina sat on the bench. Michael came over to her and started rubbing her neck. She leaned back into him. He bent down and kissed her shoulder. Before she closed her eyes, she noticed Louise, with her back to them, staring out of the window.

The windows in Bettina's apartment had been shut all winter, and when she tried to open one in the bedroom, it wouldn't budge. She stepped back, filled her cheeks with air, and blew out. The glass was smudged with nicotine and yellow cigarette tar. Her first swipe at it with the Windex and a paper towel had simply streaked the pane, so she went at it again. If she couldn't open the window just yet, she'd make sure she could at least see out of it.

The sky was the color of pewter, and the light was February gray and flat. A faded India print cloth hung folded over the rod to serve as a curtain, and in the grit of the dusty sill lay the broken shell of a horseshoe crab.

At the center of the table next to the window lay a handful of hair clippings in a neat pile, and, beside it, the long coil of braided hair, gathered at its tail and held by a red elastic band.

She would repaint. The walls were the same color they'd been when she moved in eight years earlier: a pale gray with plum mixed into it. She had already pulled the posters from the wall, and there were glaring, irregular white shapes where the masking tape had torn the paint off. They looked like soft, smooth scars, or places where someone had poked holes straight through the wall of the room and the brick wall of the building to the outside, which was all glaring and white. Before she painted, she would have to scrape. The thought of it exhausted her.

She raked her fingers over the top of her head. It still felt queer to have so little hair. She had set out to trim her bangs and kept on cutting and reached her braid. She had cut slowly, patiently, across the thick tail of hair, until the braid had begun to come loose and detach itself from her head. And once she'd gone that far, she decided to keep cutting without benefit of a mirror, using only her hands and the new light feel of her head to guide her.

There was a new lightness in her whole body since the day Louise and Michael's friend had come to the studio. It was as though she had shed something tight and cumbersome, as surely as that street woman had shed the overcoat in her vestibule, for it was entirely possible she had cast it off on purpose, let it slide down her arms, and, stepping out of the crumpled garment, been surprised to find her limbs moved freely.

It was joy that had burst in upon her that day in the studio, joy that had risen in her own body and broken through the grief, the same urgent joy, she thought, that cracks the seed husk under the soil. It was what she had longed for, the thing just out of reach, the very thing one was almost certain one dared not desire. It was, she thought, what her mother must have wanted too. And when the wall disappeared and Michael danced out into the middle of the air, surrounded by light, Bettina had stood gazing upon the thing itself, unmasked, the Truth that shone both within and far beyond the world of form. It was one's Self, the Beloved, larger than her desire for Michael, her reliance upon Louise, her work. And yet it was the very thing the work needed to contain and express—Radha's revelation—that joy.

For If He Left Robert

*F*or if he left Robert, there would be no one else; that much was clear, very clear to him, and he needed this one thing in particular to be clear in his own mind at least, because of course it was all the same to Robert, one way or another. In the end, it didn't matter much to him, but for Karl things needed to be clear, and so as he stood at the window, fingering the brass latch on the shutter—the window was open, and the light he now stood in was gray, though it was mid-morning and Robert lay on his side, curled in, facing the cracked wall of the hotel room they'd been living in for how many months now, all of the early autumn at least, maybe just a matter of weeks—and so as he fingered the brass latch on the open shutter, it struck Karl as odd, this line of thought which seemed to end so succinctly: there will be no one else after this; after this it is over for me. Which did not mean he was going to jump off one of the river bridges. He intended to go on living. It's just that he intended to live alone now, and it was now, as he stood at the window in the gray light, that he knew.

If he left Robert now, if he packed quietly and checked out of the hotel and did not leave a forwarding address, because of course he didn't have one, he couldn't see any farther in his mind than the street corner, the avenue he'd walk up to catch the Metro that would take him to Gare du Nord, where he'd board a train to Brussels—if he left Robert now, while he was still asleep, chances were that Robert wouldn't notice, that he'd wake up and call Karl's name, and, finding him not there, would stretch, hum, shave, dress, walk out of the hotel, resume his life, for it took Robert no time at all to get his bearings, to shed one attachment and pick up another, so sweet, so simple was the pleasure he found in love, the joy that rose in him as he breathed, dug his thumbnail into the skin of an orange, lifted it off, broke the flesh into sections, offered it.

So Robert would go on. He would survive this. But somehow Karl knew he himself would not, for if he left Robert, there would be no returning to this or any other hotel room where someone stretched and woke beside him, yawning, and spoke his name, no return simply because he foresaw their life together in one or two rooms at the top of a five-story house near Rue des Ursulines, in the neighborhood of the deaf school, or farther up towards Montparnasse, near the Prison de la Santé, Prison of Health (what could they have meant, to give it a name like that?), and it was not the poverty of those rooms, nor the smudged light. It was the tidiness, the brave domesticity, and especially the moments which threatened to destroy, to rend the delicate fabric, so carefully woven, of what might have been their life together: the unmade bed, a bowl of fruit perched dangerously on the windowsill, a spot on the tablecloth Karl had promised to have laundered but had forgotten to—moments, none of which he had lived, but which now sprang up in images before him as he gazed down at the floor and noticed the faint discoloration between the legs of Robert's underpants, or were they his own? The question suddenly filled him with horror, as though he had already disappeared, not of his own will, by dressing and then going out, but by being assumed into Robert (which, indeed, were his underpants, his socks?), so that when Robert awoke and took no notice of Karl's absence, it would be because Karl lived inside Robert now, and as Robert stood, admiring himself in the mirror, it was Karl's hand, now his own hand, that he ran along the smooth lean stretch of his flanks, across his belly, and down a thigh, so Karl shuddered at first and then grinned because after all, that is what he had wanted at first, what he always wanted at first, this union, to become one with another, to lose himself in, but once again, he had gone too far, and so he was pulling back into his own mind as he turned from Robert—who now lay on his belly and moved his pelvis this way and that—turned from Robert and looked out the window at a ragged bit of mist or smoke that had partially obscured a small green dome far off in the distance.

What Robert had said the night before ("Why bother yourself with politics? Why do you give a shit? It's not even your own country?"), he had said in exasperation, urging Karl away from the window and back into the bed he'd left to see where the chanting and the sirens had come from, to see if he could hear whose side the protesters were on, what words they were shouting, whether they demanded the execution of the Spanish radicals or their immediate release, to see if he could understand without pulling on his clothes and venturing out into the streets again. ("*Merde, alors! Qu'est-ce que tu as?* Why does nothing give you pleasure?" which Karl took to mean "Why aren't I enough for you?" a question Karl wanted to answer by shaking *Le Monde* in Robert's face, the front page with its photograph of students in the streets of Rome, radicals in Köln, in Nice, in Barcelona: the largest popular demonstrations in Europe since the trial of Sacco and Vanzetti.)

But there was no way Robert could understand, no way to explain it to him because he honestly thought Madrid was far away and what happened there or in Rome or even eight streets over had nothing to do with him, had nothing to do with what he called "us." At the same time, Robert had given rise to an ugly fear in Karl that perhaps the events in Madrid really didn't have much to do with them, that maybe Robert was enough, ought to be enough for him, that this was all there was, right here in a hotel room in the gray light of mid-morning, with his lover asleep on his belly, dreaming of Alpine forests and clear streams (so Karl imagined) or of the room they'd share at the top of a house near the Prison de la Santé, where (he had heard just the other morning) they were holding two German radicals with alleged connections to the Baader-Meinhof group, and for some reason he could not get it out of his mind, this Prison of Health, with two of his countrymen within its walls, two comrades perhaps (for the press was forever matching radicals with the wrong groups), but it frightened Karl even more to admit that Robert was becoming, had perhaps already become his homeland, his own country, the center of the struggle. Elsewhere, when one traveled abroad and there was a railway strike, a coal miner's strike, one had the liberty of shrugging. One could say one knew nothing about it, knew nothing of the background. While abroad, one could apologize for one's ignorance. One smiled. One said, one could be expected to say, "*Enfin, ce n'est pas mon pays;* it's not my country." One could even pretend not to understand the question, pretend not to speak the language.

But here, these past weeks, these past months had robbed him of his innocence, had engulfed him in knowledge (he now imagined he knew what Robert was dreaming), so that his ignorance was a sham, a pretense, and so if he was here, if he had crossed the line and entered this landscape, why not stay? What, after all, prevented him? A mark at the crotch of some underpants? An imagined quarrel about the placement of a bowl of fruit? The terror of disappearing into another's flesh and thoughts—though Karl needn't have worried; at the moment, Robert dreamt of a boyhood friend he'd known summers in the Midi, and now, in the dream, Robert was himself a boy wrestling with his boyhood friend by the sea (and here Karl noticed Robert moving his pelvis back and forth).

But he felt obliged, Karl did, to stay, having somehow crossed that frontier, having stepped into the new countryside, which gleamed here and there (as the sun broke through the mid-morning cloud cover), so that he felt pulled toward Robert, drawn to him just then, watching him sleep, and reached out to him as he moved toward the bed to wake him, but stopped again, remembering his resolve: to make no attempt to possess him, to keep himself from loving Robert, but then if he left Robert, there would be no one else—that much was clear—and so Karl needed to decide, one way or the other, what he was to do, and just then, as he wavered for a moment between the window and the bed, Robert woke up and smiled at him and stretched and asked for a breakfast of green apples, coffee, and thin slices of gruyère.

Hurley

*H*urley waits at the counter of The Fifth Wheel, a pornography shop, holding a suitcase in his right hand. With
his shoulders squared and his knees bent slightly, he
stands poised on the balls of his feet, as if he is about to leap
forward. The cashier has backed himself up against the glass display case so suddenly that one of the battery-operated dildos has
begun to vibrate and jars of lubricant jelly knock against each
other. Hurley has just announced, in a calm, straightforward man-
ner, that he has a bomb in his suitcase and that it's set to go off in
ten minutes.

He doesn't really have a bomb in his suitcase; it's his laundry,
and it's easier for him to get it to and from the laundromat this
way. He's been meaning to come into The Fifth Wheel for a long
time. He wants to talk to the manager or the clerk or to the cus-
tomers face to face. He thinks by talking to other men calmly and
reasonably he'll discover they are surprisingly innocent, largely
unaware of what these images of women actually mean.

Before walking up to the counter to confront the cashier, Hurley has been thumbing through the magazines, trying to decide
what to do. One magazine cover shows a woman mashing her
large breasts together and screwing up her face for a kiss. Inside
are pictures of women wearing black stockings and garter belts.
They look drunk or drugged, as if they've passed out or fallen

asleep while posing. Then he stops at a series of pictures of a young woman seated on the edge of a bathtub, drying her long hair with a towel, standing at a window full of plants, looking out, as though she were unaware that a photographer was watching her through a lens.

She looks like a girl he might have sat next to in high school civics. She is probably somebody's little sister, and he wonders what she's doing in a magazine like this. Unless her boyfriend has sold the pictures without her knowing about it. Or she is a young housewife from the suburbs with a secret life in the city. Or a revolutionary, posing as a model, but really gathering information for the radical press. He likes to imagine her putting finely ground glass in the cocaine she later serves to the Pornography King. After all, he thinks, Emma Goldman once posed as a prostitute to earn money for a gun she would need to assassinate an industrialist. Why not?

The man behind the counter has flattened his back against the glass of the display case. He works his mouth around as if he is trying to reconnect his jaw without using his hands. He lunges forward, punches a button on the register, grabs handfuls of bills, checks, and Mastercard slips out of the open drawer, and waves them in Hurley's face.

"Take it. Take it all," he says. "You want fuck books? They're behind you. Videos? They're in the corner. I got one—a guy's doing it with an ostrich. Take it. Take anything you want. Just get out of here."

Hurley smiles and shakes his head. He tries to get the cashier to understand what he means by the difference between erotica and violence against women. He points to the picture in the magazine that lies open on the counter. It shows a woman, bound and gagged. She is naked, and a man wearing army fatigues has stuck the barrel of an M-16 into her vagina.

"This," says Hurley, "is what I mean."

The man behind the counter stuffs the money back into the cash drawer and turns to the phone on his left. Hurley reaches across the counter, grabs the man's shoulder, and says, "No. You don't understand."

"I understand plenty," says the man. "You're a lunatic, and I'm calling the police."

It's clear to Hurley that the man is not interested in any sort of meaningful political dialogue, so he closes the magazine, puts it under his arm, picks up his suitcase, and leaves.

There is hardly anybody in the laundromat. Hurley puts his clothes right into a machine, sits down on the far end of a bench that runs along the wall, and opens the magazine to the pictures of the beautiful woman drying her hair. If the man at the bookstore had given him the chance, he would have shown him that not all photographs of women were violent. At the same time, Hurley's feeling about the pictures is so strong and so private, he's glad he has kept them to himself.

On the other end of the bench sits a woman wearing a red peasant blouse with what looks like lingerie lace sewn onto the border of the scoop-neck collar, and a red and white checked gingham skirt that makes him think of a tablecloth in a diner. On her head, she wears a baseball cap with a flesh-colored hand coming out of the front of it, holding a steel-colored gun, which wags back and forth each time she moves her head to a tune Hurley can't hear because she's wearing earphones. She looks like she has something in her eye or a facial tic, but she grins, and Hurley realizes she's been winking at him. He smiles, gives her a quick nod, closes the magazine on his lap, and spots the morning paper lying close by on the bench.

The picture on the front page shows a man leaning out a window. In his left hand he holds a baby by the feet. In his right hand, a knife. The man looks down at the street, away from the baby. The article explains that the man has taken his two–year-old son hostage after arguing with his wife about custody. The journalist describes the man as a "distraught father," but the man doesn't look distraught. He doesn't look like he's going to drop the baby. He looks like he is posing. The baby, however, does not look posed. His mouth is open, and his small body curls toward the window, his left arm outstretched, reaching for the man who is using him as a prop.

Hurley eyes the photograph coolly. He is training himself not to be afraid. He stares at the square black letters of the headline. He stares and waits for the moment of terror to pass. Often, while standing in line at the drugstore to buy a newspaper, the fear is so strong in him that he is almost sure other people can smell it, the way dogs can smell if you're afraid of them. So he always folds the newspaper under his arm, tosses his thirty cents on the counter, and walks back to his room at the YMCA, where he can be alone with it for a while, and after reading the article over, and studying the pictures, he grows less and less afraid, and throws the paper onto the pile in the dustiest corner of his room.

This morning, it is pretty easy. He has faced the headlines, looked at the picture right there in the laundromat, and he has not exuded that smell. Even if he has, there's no one there to smell it—no one dangerous. The woman at the far end of the bench has forgotten all about him and is moving her head back and forth, smiling to the tune on her radio.

Once he has packed his clean clothes neatly into his suitcase, he folds the newspaper around the girlie magazine, puts them both under his arm, and heads home.

Hurley stands at a corner, waiting for the light to change. When the traffic light turns green, a figure lights up in a little box for pedestrians. It's supposed to look like someone walking, but it looks to Hurley like the line the police draw around a body that has landed on the sidewalk after a fall from a twelfth-story window, the body of someone who's been stabbed or shot down and left lying in the street, or the shapes that protesters stencil on the sidewalks each year on the anniversary of Hiroshima to commemorate the shadows that were burned into the pavement.

Up ahead of him on Congress Street, he sees a tiny woman wearing a beige coat and a bright orange hat. She is scraping the notices for rock concerts and religious revivals off a lamp post with a key. She moves her hand in short, rapid little motions, scraping a long time on one square inch to make sure she gets all the paper off because the glue is so strong. Hurley stops a few paces away from the woman and puts his suitcase down, relieved. She's doing a fine job and he wants to tell her so. He likes it that people get it into their heads to do what others wouldn't think to do, and it's a service to the community. She's helping to keep the city lamp posts clean, free of charge. He's afraid that talking to her will scare her away, so he takes his room key from his pocket and steps forward to start scraping the notices off the other side. In that way, he hopes to strike up a conversation.

But just then, someone's head hits him right between the shoulder blades, and he hears four or five aluminum cans bouncing on the sidewalk all around him. Hurley turns to face a small, fierce-looking brown woman who carries a potato sack and hollers at him in Spanish. He doesn't understand a word, but he apologizes and leans over to help the woman pick up the cans. The small woman leaps up at him, places her hands on his shoulders, and shoves him hard, which sends him stumbling backward over his suitcase and lands him on his back. He sits up, blinks, rubs his shoulder, and explains to the woman that he's not stealing her cans, which he knows are worth a nickel apiece.

All three of them—Hurley, the Spanish woman, and the woman scraping paper off the lamp post—see the policeman at the same time.

"Now you've done it," hisses the lamp post woman, pointing her key at Hurley and narrowing her eyes.

Hurley jumps up, brushes off his trousers, and stands his suitcase upright again. The Spanish woman is just putting the last cans back into her sack when the policeman reaches them.

"Everything all right?" he asks.

"Yes, officer," says Hurley as he raises his right arm to draw attention to the old woman. "We bumped into each other, but we're fine. Nobody's hurt." He looks again at the Spanish woman to see if this is true. She nods at the policeman, points to the sky, and talks very quickly about Maria, La Maria Negra. Then she curtsies and starts bowing at the waist. "*Gracias señor, señora,*" she says. "*Gracias a Dios. Adiós,*" she says as she backs up, bowing again, and scoots into an alley. By now Hurley has picked up his suitcase, crossed the street, and is walking in the door of Paul's Ghetto Market. The woman at the lamp post resumes her scraping.

Once inside the grocery store, Hurley tries to imagine what will happen if he tells one of the cashiers he has a bomb in his suitcase. She might panic and call the manager. He likes to think that people standing in line will spread the word and start looting immediately. The people with full shopping carts waiting to pay will push right past the cashiers and wheel their carts into the street.

Mothers who are careful to compare the price of chicken and fish will head straight for the steaks and start tossing them into their baskets, while their kids run and grab all the Doritos and M&Ms they can carry. Old men will grab bottles of wine off the shelf and cold beer out of the cooler, laughing and singing, and fat people who've been looking at the Weight Watchers Gourmet Frozen Dinners will start leaping towards the ice cream.

Hurley wonders where he'd plant a bomb if he had one. If he put it up front, near the window, the damage would catch the attention of people in the street, but he'd have to worry about the flying glass. He doesn't want anyone to get hurt. Besides, if he blows up the freezers at the back of the store, he'll put Paul's Ghetto Market out of commission, and chances are they'll keep the story in the papers for quite a while. Or the dairy section. He likes the idea of all that milk, yogurt, and cottage cheese exploding.

Which reminds him of what he's come into the grocery store to get in the first place: strawberry yogurt and a quart of milk. He is midway down the produce aisle, on his way to the dairy section, when a ball of damp, brown lettuce flies over his left shoulder. He turns and sees two old ladies facing off, shouting at each other. One is a bag lady. The other looks like a retired librarian. They wear identical charcoal gray and white checkerboard tweed coats. The librarian probably bought hers twenty years ago on sale at Peck & Peck, and has taken good care of it, sending it to the dry cleaner once a year and mending the lining when it wears out. It's obvious that the bag lady bought hers at the Salvation Army or St. Joseph the Provider, and while there's no telling what kind of shape it was in when she bought it, it is now soiled and torn and ratty.

"I'm sorry, madam, but I saw it first. That was *my* head of lettuce," says the librarian.

"Like hell it was," cries the bag lady. "I had my hand on it, and you grabbed it away from me." She picks up another head of lettuce and shakes it in the librarian's face. The librarian notices that the lettuce is greener than any of the others in the bin, so she tries to snatch it out of the bag lady's hand, but the lettuce falls apart around their feet. The bag lady is about to kick the librarian in the shin when Hurley steps in and shouts, "Stop. Stop fighting each other."

"It's none of your damn business," hollers the bag lady. "It's between her and me, so you just butt out, why don't you."

"You don't understand," cries Hurley. "It's useless to fight each other when your real fight is with the owner of the store. He's the one responsible for the high prices and the rotten produce. He's the one who profits."

The librarian has been sucking her top lip, trying to screw up her courage. She finally slaps the bag lady hard across the face and darts behind Hurley for protection.

"Now stop it. Both of you," says Hurley.

The bag lady glares past Hurley's head at the librarian, who makes a face at her and sticks out her tongue. Then the librarian smiles at Hurley, pats his arm, and tells him to get the manager to have this filthy woman removed from the premises.

A drunk, who's been slipping bottles of vanilla into the pockets of his overcoat and who's seen the whole thing, sneaks up behind the librarian, grabs her around the waist, and starts dragging her back down the aisle towards the cake mixes. He knows the bag lady. She's a friend of his. The librarian flails her arms and shouts and kicks over a display pile of canned generic cat food. The cans start to bounce and roll up and down the aisle, so that when the manager, who wears a green jacket with his name embroidered on the right breast pocket, rounds the corner to see what all the commotion is about, he has to step deftly to keep from falling over.

Hurley holds the bag lady away from him at arm's length. He's been trying to explain to her some of the larger issues of food production and distribution under capitalism. She kicks and punches at him, cursing under her breath, "Communist punk. Buttinski. Meddler."

The manager comes up, takes the bag lady from Hurley, turns her around to face him, and says, "Now Judy. Didn't I tell you last time you weren't to shop here anymore if you couldn't behave yourself? Look at the mess you've made. I should call the police, but I'm going to give you one more chance. I don't want to see you around here for a while, OK?"

The bag lady opens her mouth to blame it on the librarian, but thinks better of it, turns, and walks toward the door, muttering to herself.

Hurley turns to pick up his suitcase and finds the girlie magazine lying open to the picture of the woman sitting on the edge of her bathtub. He leans over, folds it back into the newspaper, and shoves them both under his arm. When he stands up again, the manager is leering at him. He winks at Hurley and walks off to save the librarian.

With his suitcase clutched firmly in his right hand, and the newspaper and girlie magazine pressed under his left armpit, Hurley walks back up the produce aisle and out the door.

Back in his room, Hurley lies on his narrow army cot and fingers the smooth border of the pillowcase because it makes him feel safe. He has been trying to sleep, but his left eye is twitching. He has come home, lifted weights for an hour, taken a long hot shower. He has done everything he can think of, but still he is afraid, and so he stares up at the yellowing ceiling, until it seems to be descending slowly along the green walls, which also seem to be moving in on him, though it is impossible, just as it is impossible that his heart has been shrinking, even though he is pretty sure it has, because of the salt in his diet maybe.

Everything in the streets today, in the grocery store, everything in the hallways of the Y, in the weight room and in the showers, is menacing. Even sex seems poisonous to him. He has walked slowly up to his room after his workout, locked the door, and opened his magazine to the picture of the woman drying her hair, trying to feel what he had felt for her in the bookstore, but twenty minutes later, after he has wiped the sperm from his belly and pulled his trousers back up, he is ashamed. He has used her— this woman who might be a revolutionary, this woman with her own interior life, her own glory and her own fears—he has used the images of her in ways she herself has no say about, in ways he hasn't meant or wanted to. The woman in the picture no longer has reality for him, and he feels more alone than ever. He wants to talk to her. He wants to apologize, but that's impossible, so he lies on his bed, staring up at the ceiling, trying to make his left eye stop twitching. He runs his thumb over the smooth border of his pillowcase, so he will feel less afraid.

At sunset, Hurley sits on the floor of his room with a pair of scissors in his right hand and a newspaper in his left. He has grabbed it off the pile that's over a foot high in the corner, and he cuts out an article about a woman in New York City who put her eighteen-month-old son in an oven to drive the devil out of him. There's a picture of the boy's father, snapped just as he's been told what has happened. His shoulders are hunched over, his palms outstretched and turned up to the air, his face caught in a grimace, the mouth open, eyes cast upward, as if he were shouting at God.

Hurley wonders what it's like to be the boy's father and to be told that his son has been roasted in an oven. He wonders what it's like to have your face clench into that expression, so he imitates it, pulling his mouth into a grin, breathing in through his teeth, then opening his mouth slightly, as if he were saying "Ah." Hurley goes to the mirror that hangs on a nail above his bureau and holds the newspaper picture next to his face to see how closely he can match the expression. Then he bends over, sticking his right hand out in front of him, but it's useless. He can't look up at heaven and into the mirror at the same time, so he goes back and sits on the floor next to the stack of old newspapers.

He has read where the woman, after closing the oven door on her son, was heard chanting by a neighbor. He wonders what she chanted, and whether or not she rocked back and forth in her wooden chair in the kitchen, as Hurley now rocks back and forth on the floor of his room.

He tries hard not to think about what it's like to be the little boy, lying in the dark, hot oven, smelling the grease, reaching to touch the wall with its baked-on food.

Hurley cuts slowly, evenly through the newsprint to the right of a column of words, and once he has finished pastes it into a cardboard-bound laboratory notebook with graph-paper pages that make it easier to line up the clippings. He has over seventy notebooks in all, and he keeps them locked in strongboxes on the floor of his clothes closet and at the bottom of his footlocker, tucked in a back corner, underneath his extra blanket. He has tried many different kinds of notebooks with different kinds of paper and several kinds of paste. He likes the kind he's using now. Some of the clippings in the older notebooks have come unstuck, the brittle, yellowing newsprint has started to lift off the pages, so he'll have to go back and reglue them, which makes him think of the woman in the bright orange hat who scrapes the public notices off the lamp post, and what kind of glue people use to stick them on.

He likes the sound the pages make when he flips through them and the dry, yellow smell of the newsprint. He likes the heft

and weight of a notebook once he's finished it, and sometimes
he spends a whole Sunday afternoon rereading the articles he's
pasted into the books, satisfied that one event follows another
in sequence—an earthquake in Chile comes after a chain-saw
murder in northern Maine—so that by twilight the world makes
some kind of sense to him, though by the next morning he can't
remember how or why.

What Do You Mean
What Am I Doing?

*W*hat do you think I am doing? What does it look like I am doing? I am sitting here in my old dirty bathrobe, singing an old sweet song. That is, I am trying to. There are two problems. The first is you sitting there asking me what I am doing. It breaks my concentration. The second is that I cannot quite remember all the words to the song I am trying to sing. Or the right melody either. I keep getting it all mixed up with *Wish You Were Here*. Wasn't that the title of it? Or *Now You Are Here and I Am Gone*. No. I don't think anybody ever wrote a song and called it that.

And if you would quit staring at me, I could get on with it.

No! Leave the light off. I cannot hang on to the mood I am after, and if I am not in the right mood, the song, . . . well, the song . . . I get it all messed up.

Now where was I?

Now you are here and I am gone. You know what, I bet nobody ever did write a song like that. And I reckon it's time somebody did. Because you know something? That is how I am getting to feel these days. Wish I Was Gone.

I hate it when you come in here like that.

Why can't you have dropped dead like I thought you might have waiting for you five hours ago?

Here You Are, and Oh My Darling Now I'm Gone.

That's the real tune, but I don't think the words are right.

I do not want to hear where you were. I don't care. I think I cared earlier this evening—much earlier. In fact so much earlier it may have been yesterday evening. How long *have* you been gone?

Now that's got to be a song.

I told you. I don't want to hear it. Do not. Do you understand plain English?

It is my rabbit fur hat with the earflaps that pull down and tie under my chin. I am pulling the earflaps down at the moment, so I can concentrate on my music.

I know what month it is. I am not wearing it because of the weather. It is on my head to facilitate my art. A thing about which you understand exactly nothing.

Pardon me?

I am picking out the tune on my piano.

I know this is not a piano. I am fully aware of the fact that this is a table. Do you think I have gone and lost my mind? Honestly. Shhh.

I am trying to concentrate. You are too damn literal, you know? That's your trouble. One of them. One of several.

What?

I don't have to tell you. If you wanted me to tell you your problems, you'd have been here five hours ago or yesterday or last week, whenever it was you were supposed to be here and were *not*.

My clothes? I have retired for the evening. And you are not supposed to be here.

You always do this.

Now shush. Quit interrupting. I've lost my place. I'm trying to get this right.

What!

What do you mean doing to myself? Do I look like I'm *doing* anything to myself? My bathrobe is closed. My hands are right here on the piano. Not a bit of funny business. I have my rabbit fur hat right here on the top of my head, and the earflaps are pulled down. It's real rabbit. A gift from a former admirer. Real live rabbit. It says so on the label. And someday if you ever arrive when you say you're going to arrive, I might show it to you.

Now, if you'll excuse me, I'll get back to what I was doing.

What was I doing? Oh I know. Picking out this tune on my good old piano. A Steinway: the Cadillac of pianos.

All right, then. Leave. Nobody asked you to come barging in here in the middle of the night to distract me from what I was doing. Of course, you said you were coming over some time ago, and when it was clear that you were not going to be coming, then I set about to occupy myself with something else. Idle hands are the devil's hobgoblins. Is that how it goes?

What do you mean it's only nine o'clock? It's got to be more than nine o'clock. I've been sitting here for hours. What do you know? It is only nine o'clock. P.M. not A.M., right? How time flies when you've been sitting someplace for hours.

Have I had dinner?

Maybe not. And if that's the case, let's go out. I'll just slip off this dirty old bathrobe and slip into something less comfortable, a pair of dirty old slacks and a dirty old coat and tie. And we'll go out.

I don't know. What day is it?

Oh Sunday. You're right. Sunday. Yes, I see.

OK, then here's what I think. I think you ought to sit back

down. Fix yourself a drink. Sure! Let's get drunk. If you start right now, I bet you could catch up to me in about three days.

On your mark. Get set . . .

Oh all right, be that way, you old stick in the shit.

OK. You're leaving. So what else is new? I can't remember the last time you showed up, much less stayed a while.

And I'm warning you. It is a known fact that neglected lovers often turn to someone else for solace. So do not make me be unfaithful. It'd ruin my record. Which is perfect, in case you hadn't noticed.

So get out, then. Who needs you? I shall just get back to what I was trying to remember before you interrupted me.

Sure you will. *Pick Up the Phone and Just Call Me.* I remember that one. Petula Clark, right?

OK. Bye.

. . .

Now you're gone, and oh my darlin' I'm gone too.

. . .

Asshole.

Ralph and Larry

I once met a guy who said he'd given Allen Ginsberg a blow job after a poetry reading in Gettysburg, Pennsylvania. Ralph says that distinguishes me from everyone else he's ever known. That and the fact I managed to—as Ralph puts it—eat my way into Renard, the psychiatric ward of Barnes Hospital here in St. Louis. What happened was I got depressed and had to be hospitalized. Ralph is referring to what happened right before I was admitted, an incident which ruined my prospects for a career.

I met Ralph when I was in Renard. He was an orderly. In those days he wanted to be a psychiatric nurse, but he decided to make money, real money, so he took business courses at Forest Park Community College, and now he's a claims adjuster for a life insurance company, I better not say which one. I always picture him adjusting things, making things adjust—numbers mostly, I guess. It's the perfect job for him. He likes to get things right. He used to try to get me right, but he never had much luck, so it's important that he get something right, somewhere, and the insurance company's usually where he does it.

The reason I best not say which company he works for is he's a sadist. First he turned gay, that was one thing, but this is quite another. Hardly anybody bats an eye these days if you're gay, but sadism can still make some people, well, nervous. Shoot, it can make a lot of people downright queasy. I can't say I was thrilled when Ralph told me, but I figure he's stuck by me all these years with all I've been through, the least I could do was to stick by him through this. And you never know with Ralph. This might just be a phase.

I really ought to go and let him out. I left him over an hour ago.

When Ralph turned gay, he thought I should turn gay too. He even took me to that bar in the Central West End one night. What a disaster! It was the middle of July, and the air conditioning was broken. The place was packed, so the ceiling fans didn't do much good, and it was loud. I mean LOUD. And I wasn't supposed to drink because of my medication—I might have still been on thorazine at that point, though I think they had me on lithium and cogentin as an experiment—but whatever I was on was drying out my mouth, so I kept drinking glass after glass of water, which made me have to pee all the time, so I had to go back and forth, back and forth to the men's room, and when you're as big as I am, it's quite a chore.

I won't even attempt to describe to you what all was going on in the men's room.

Ralph says it'd make all the difference in the world if I could stand naked and look down and see my genitals without first having to lift my belly out of the way. He says I'd feel easier about exploring my sexuality if I could find my sex. Now I have nothing whatsoever against sex, gay or straight, I'm just not interested. I'm neutral, like Switzerland.

And almost as big. I'm fat. Real fat. Ralph is a slight, dapper little man. Everything about him seems in perfect proportion. The only thing that interrupts is the hearing aid he wears in his left ear, which I almost forget is there most times, except when he reaches up to adjust it or turn it off when it whines. Suddenly this weird noise just starts up out of nowhere, and I remember it's Ralph's hearing aid. It's especially bad in late summer, when the locusts are out, and we'll be sitting outside and his hearing aid will be tuned to human conversation, and then he'll pick up the locusts and the thing goes wild, whirring and buzzing, it sounds like a locust must have flown right into his brain and is trying to get out by the ear, so then he bangs the side of his head and turns it down, but then it might be too low to pick up human conversation again.

Me? I hear just fine. Ralph says I'm a good listener. But there's nothing small or dapper about me. I'm fat, fat, fat. Right now I'm holding steady at 418 pounds, but I've been bigger. Sure, everybody tells you it's the thyroid, and it is, but I also love to eat. Food is one of the only things in life I take seriously. My mother never was much of a cook, so it was up to me to learn how to do it myself. And my psychiatrist, Dr. Post, has helped me to understand how that has shaped my whole life. Ha! Just look at me!

When I go over to Ralph's house—and I better get back pretty soon or he's going to be furious—I always sit in his La-Z-Boy recliner. Other than the sofa, it's the only piece of furniture he's got that will hold me. From there, I can see into the kitchen, and earlier this afternoon I noticed something was different about the counter. It took me a minute to think what it was, but then I saw that Ralph had replaced the red and white quilted covers for his toaster and Mixmaster with brown ones that looked to be made of leather. And they matched, which made me think they'd come with brown leather pot holders and a suede tea towel. That tickled me, and I commenced to chuckle, but when Ralph said, "What's so funny?" I said, "Never mind," because it was clear to me, the way he asked, he was in no mood for trifling, so I just kept on eating my piece of strawberry rhubarb pie a la mode. Ralph still makes great pies.

Ralph was irritated because he was trying to assemble a whole mess of long, black leather straps into what he said was some kind of halter, but believe you me, it didn't look like anything you'd want to try and put on a horse. Ralph explained that you hung it from the ceiling and strapped your sex partner into it so as he couldn't move.

"What in the world would anyone want to do that for?" I asked.

"It's to heighten the pleasure" was all he said.

"Oh," I said and finished my pie.

I returned the La-Z-Boy recliner to its upright position, hefted myself out of it, and went to the kitchen for another piece. When I opened the icebox door, Ralph said, "Why don't you ask first, Larry?" but without any real conviction. Besides, I had already lifted the last piece of pie out of the glass plate and put it on my own. "You weren't saving it, were you?" I hollered. "It'll just get stale, Ralph, and then you'll throw it away." I had my hand on the freezer door when I remembered. "Hey Ralph," I said, "did you know you're out of ice cream? I'll put it on your list, so you can get some when you go to the store."

"Jesus," said Ralph under his breath.

I eased myself back into the recliner, balancing my plate on my knees. Ralph tightened the nut on a bolt, securing the end of a leather strip that looped through a steel ring.

"It's bad for your heart," he said, "carrying around all that weight. You should get some exercise, eat something other than valium and pies."

I looked up from my plate for a moment. I watched him attach the other end of the leather strip to a silvery ring. I looked back down at my plate. I picked up my fork.

As I say, Ralph has this perfect job, adjusting and correcting and telling people how things ought to be. I used to think I had the perfect job until I lost it. The job turned out to be dangerous. A lot of people got hurt. I mean emotionally. That was how I got hospitalized. I was in the catering business. I studied in Paris. Now that I think back, the trouble started in that restaurant in Vienna, the one that hired me after I worked under the pastry chef at the American embassy. I mean I always picked. That was natural. A taste of this, a taste of that, to make sure it was right. But all of a sudden I'd be placing a sprig of parsley on an expensive dish of food, just so, and I'd look down and there'd be a bite out of the duck, and I'd be chewing. Even so, I didn't make the connection at first. I'd just turn the duck to hide the bitten-out part, or remold the mound of wild rice to erase the impression of my nose. All without anyone seeing. Until one, and then another, customer complained.

Later, Dr. Post helped me to see that as the danger increased so did the frequency of my unconscious attacks on the plates of food. Deep down inside, I wanted to get caught. It was a cry for help. One night a waitress came back to pick up an order. She took one look at the plate and just stared at me. "I can't serve this; it's half eaten!" When I went to scratch my face, I noticed I had béarnaise sauce all over my chin. Without even then fully realizing what had happened, I made up a new plate.

When I moved back to St. Louis, my mother had prepared the way by talking to her sister, my Aunt Bert, who talked to a lady she knew in the Wednesday Club whose daughter was a debutante who had recently gone to a dinner dance catered by a new company formed by people my own age who'd all gone to hotsy-totsy Eastern boarding schools together, and whom I knew vaguely from parties during the Christmas holidays growing up. Anyway, it was arranged that I talk to them. And, I don't know, I had a certain air about me when I moved back from Europe, self-confidence I suppose, and they liked what they saw, and they especially liked my training and the food I prepared for them. So they hired me as a chef.

It was about six months later, the night of the Queen's Supper after the Veiled Prophet Ball—the absolute most important social event of the entire year; I mean you do a good job on this one, everybody talks, and you've got work for a long time to come— it was at the Queen's Supper that I ruined my career not only as a caterer but also as a chef and, as Ralph puts it, ate my way into Renard.

To this day, I cannot remember what happened. I didn't come to until a few days later, and I was still under restraint. Ralph was on duty the night I was admitted. He was the one who had to restrain me. He may be small, but he's strong. Later he told me the *Post Dispatch* said when the guests began to file into the Khorasan Room of the Chase Park Plaza Hotel they saw a very fat man in a white apron writhing along the top of a buffet table covered in white satin and festooned with orchids and purple velvet bunting. According to one eyewitness, I was digging my pelvis into the liver paté, with my face buried in the front steps of a scale model of the Old Court House sculpted in Alaska salmon. The reporter from the *Globe* was kind enough to say it was a miracle I didn't suffocate. And when you get right down to it, the members of the Order and the guests of His Mysterious Majesty, the Veiled Prophet, showed me every kindness by not lynching me on the spot. They called the police instead. Then somebody called an ambulance.

When I finished eating the last piece of Ralph's strawberry rhubarb pie, I watched him assembling this halter thing and thought how he was changing, and how I didn't much like what he was changing into. It's like his apartment is being drained of color. More and more things are made of leather—the pillows on the sofa, the shade on the floor lamp. Sometimes I wonder what's next, leather wallpaper? When I try to picture it, all I see is a padded cell, like the "quiet room" at Renard, a whole room upholstered in dead flesh.

Then I thought, isn't it funny how the first piece of pie always tastes better than the second?

"There," said Ralph. He picked up the finished halter and shook it once, hard, so the metal rings clanked together. "Can you give me a hand?"

"Sure," I said and followed him into the bedroom.

First we moved the bed out of the way, and Ralph climbed onto a chair to screw in the large hooks that would secure the halter to the ceiling. A thin line of plaster dust began to fall onto his sleeve, and I sneezed. Then Ralph got down and said, "Well, what do you think?"

I said it looked like some kind of weird jockstrap.

Ralph liked that.

Really what it brought to my mind was a hammock or a cradle. It smelled like a new pair of shoes. The leather strips were thick and stiff and stained with black lacquer.

Ralph grinned and rubbed his hands together.

When I was a little boy, my mother used to make me eat a one-pound steak for supper. She'd promise me a lemon meringue pie if I ate every bit of meat. I'd struggle to finish, chewing each mouthful slowly, so there'd be room for the pie when I was done. Then I'd run to the icebox and open the door. It was never there. My mother would be laughing and cackling in the other room, just beside herself. I can't tell you how often I fell for it. That's the only real experience I've had with sadism. At least in my opinion it was sadistic. I mean it was *beyond* unkind.

Ralph says leather sex has nothing to do with all that. He says it's about power. He says it makes him feel great: masters, bondage, discipline. I don't know. None of it sits quite right with me somehow. But then Ralph's never had any mental problems, never been sick a day in his life, and here I sit, big as I am, feeling more often than not like my nerves have been scraped so raw they twitch in a breeze. It's almost unbearable sometimes, being around healthy people.

Dr. Post says it might be time for me to go out and find some part-time work, so I can meet people and feel useful to society. I am not interested in being useful to society. I tell him I'm fine as I am. Just staying out of the hospital the last five years is good enough for me. Besides, I have an income. I live off the interest from a trust fund my father's family set up for me. So why should I go out there and steal a job from somebody who really needs one? I have to explain to Dr. Post over and over again that working makes me nervous, and when I get nervous I need more valium, and he's already afraid I'm becoming dependent, overly dependent, upon my medication. Oh, if that poor man only knew! Sometimes I think what keeps me mentally stable is trying to protect my analyst from learning the truth about me for all the unseemly truths about him we'd unearth in the process. He's a very fragile man, really. His hold on reality is sometimes quite . . . well. That's the way I see it. I know what I'm doing, and I don't intend to go to work.

When I tell Dr. Post about Ralph, I watch his face to see if his tic doesn't start up or if he doesn't cough. He coughs when he's irritated or frightened or upset about something. It's not a real cough from the lungs; it's a throaty cough, which he tries to make sound to be on purpose, like he's clearing his throat, but it's quite involuntary. And I've noticed he always crosses his legs, left over right, twisting to face me over his broad thigh when I talk about Ralph. I don't think Dr. Post likes Ralph, yet he doesn't forbid me to see him, because if it weren't for Ralph I'd never see anybody but my mother. And Dr. Post hates it when the only person I see is my mother.

So when I tell him about Ralph, as I said, he coughs, and then he asks me how I feel. It's funny. I'm not at all interested at that point in how I feel. I'm much more interested in seeing if I can guess what Dr. Post is feeling. And then he urges me to talk freely about my sex life. Well, that's a laugh. I don't have one. So I tell him about Ralph's, and he seems to think that's good enough. He hmmms. He ah haaas. He says, "Yes, I see," but I don't think he sees a thing. He has a notion I get turned on by Ralph's sex life, but I think it's Dr. Post that gets the thrill. I notice his interest picks right up, and if I go a few weeks without mentioning Ralph, Dr. Post asks about him. "Do you still see that friend of yours?" he says. "Oh yeah, sure," I say, and then I let loose with one of Ralph's exploits in Forest Park.

Once I told Dr. Post about Ralph's initiation into the sadomaso-chists. When Ralph told me the name of the group, I got scared he was getting hooked up with the Ku Klux Klan. But he said the Mississippi Levee Masters have nothing to do with the Klan. He said they even let some of the black men assume positions of leadership. He said their treasurer was a well-respected Negro physician. What do you bet he's a gynecologist? My mother says every male gynecologist is a sadist.

There are two things my mother does not have time for: the medical profession and the male of the species, and when you put them together—watch out. She hates men because when my father deserted her, it ruined her life. And it did, if you look at it one way. He took off, and she had to wait a long time before she could get a divorce. Then she had to take my father's family to court to get money. They were sort of prominent, and you figure it was bad enough getting a divorce in 1953, but suing your husband's family, them being who they are and all—and then *winning* . . . well.

So we were kind of on the edge of respectability, you might say, which my mother did not help a bit by driving around in a cherry red Thunderbird convertible with the golf or tennis pro of every single country club in St. Louis County. She used to drop them off at work. Made everybody furious. She was what in those days they called "fast," and there were people worried about me as a little boy. As I say, my father's family set up a trust fund for me which my mother couldn't touch. But we stuck together, Mother and I. We had to. There was no one else to stick together with.

And she did her best. She used to rent full-length color movies on my birthday to entice all the children from families she wanted to win over or get back at. Some of the children even showed up, their parents felt sorry for us, and every once in a while I'd be invited out to the Fireman's Rodeo or the Policeman's Circus with some of the children in my class at school. Mother would always leave me at the door and wave at the other grown-ups from the car; otherwise, they'd smell the liquor on her breath. She was afraid she was becoming a social liability for me. She always thought her whiskey voice made her sound like Lauren Bacall, but, to tell you the truth, she sounded more like Louis Armstrong.

So anyway, Ralph's initiation into the Mississippi Levee Masters went like this. First they put a black muslin sack over his head, like it was a hanging. At least, that's what I'd have thought. Then they led him into a van and stripped him naked. Ralph said he could feel a deep-pile plush rug on the floor and walls. He didn't guess there were any windows. He said it smelled damp and mildewy inside, like a locker room.

They drove him all the way to Kansas City and back—Ralph didn't find that out till later—and every Levee Master had his way with him, you might say. Ralph said he had things done to him, well, that I had trouble picturing. He said he lost his hearing aid. All I could think of was poor old Ralph getting so banged around in the van that his hearing aid fell out. Then I was a little relieved. I figured he couldn't hear the chains or the whistling of the leather strap or the grunts and moans of the sadist at his rump, or the grind of the axle or the driver up front stripping the gears, or the siren of an ambulance far off on a country road. He might not have heard the hot breath and the curses, or he may have heard them only as whispers, as muffled . . . sweet . . . nothings.

Dr. Post took a long time clearing his throat.

"I see you're pretty upset by this," he said.

And I was. I was crying. But I wanted to yell at Dr. Post. I wanted him to admit how upset *he* was. It's the only time I recall in five years that I've wanted to lash out at him. Of course I didn't. He'd have put me back in the hospital, and I couldn't stand the thought of being on a locked ward again. So I just went on crying quietly for the rest of the hour. Then I went home.

When Ralph finished hooking the halter up to his bedroom ceiling, he said, "Well, let's try it out." I looked at him. I said, "You mean me?" "Shoot, no," he said, "you'd pull the whole thing down, probably break your neck, and I don't have renters' insurance."

It hurt me to think he imagined I'd sue him.

I helped him move his bed back underneath the halter. Then he got up and sat in the halter, carefully at first, jiggling up and down a little with one foot still on the bed to see if the halter would hold his weight. So far, so good. Then he leaned back. The leather creaked. The halter moved back and forth a little. I held my breath. Ralph grinned after a moment and let his head rest on the little leather pillow. I guess he figured it was secure because he wrapped one of the bands around his wrist and buckled it shut. Then he asked me to fasten the other one.

Ralph closed his eyes. I think he wished I was someone else.

Even just watching all this work had given me an appetite. I had a yen for a piece of that lemon meringue pie they serve here at the diner around the corner from Ralph's building. The desire was so strong, I just turned around and walked to the living room.

"Larry!" Ralph called out. "Where are you going?"

I couldn't even say. I just had to scoot. I didn't want him to start lecturing me.

"Larry!" he cried. "Wait! Unbuckle the straps. Let me out of this thing."

But I couldn't stop. When I get a craving like this, I've got to move. It's like it takes over and won't quit until I give it something good to eat.

I fetched my sweater. "I'll be back in a second, Ralph. I've got to go on a quick errand. It's an emergency. Just stay put."

I shut the front door as Ralph hollered louder and louder, calling me all kinds of unmentionable names. And you know, it's funny. Ralph doesn't usually lose his temper. That's what made him so good at the hospital, and I suppose that's what makes him such a good claims adjuster: he's practically unflappable.

I really should go back. Like I say, it's been over an hour. But then again, I might just as well have another little piece of pie. Honestly, I can't resist lemon meringue. I hope Ralph makes lemon meringue next. He hasn't made it in a long, long time.

I wonder if that's not why I hang around him so much—that he makes those pies, and my mother never did.

Beauty and the Beast

para todas las desaparecidas
(for all of the disappeared)

*I*n the dream, you lie on top of me, asleep. Your shoulder presses down on my breastbone. You have me pinned, I turn my head, I strain my neck to keep breathing. In the dream, I know I must get myself out from under you without waking you, or you will kill me. I finger the fur on your back, shaping it into wings I pray will lift you away from my face, lift you off the face of the earth, so I can breathe the air that opens between us, breathe deep and unimpeded.

I wake from the dream. You lie on top of me, asleep. I am startled awake by the dream itself and by the effort to breathe— easier now that I've moved and your shoulder no longer lies over my throat. I can move no farther; my hair is caught in your claw.

In the dream, the faces of my two elder sisters float up behind your head, laughing, laughing and urging you on, urging you into me, though I cannot bear the pain of you, cannot bear your pain inside me.

Awake, I consider my father. When I came here, I was ready

to die to save him. That was the agreement: my life for his. But somehow it has fallen upon me to save you both, keep you both alive. It seems my death is no longer called for. Instead, this is. Lying under you. Here. Trying to breathe.

In the dream, you and I wrestle on bedrock. All of the topsoil and loam has been scraped away by our struggle, which is and is not the usual struggle. Between man and beast. Woman and man. Most simply call it love.

Dried blood mats the fur on your neck. I notice it has streamed down your chest. I am only half awake, and for a moment I think it's mine. Then I know it's the blood of a fawn or doe you've eaten in the woods. It has dried over everything. It has a crusty smell. And then I think it is yours. You are dead. But no. You still breathe, the ribs expand, your back rises and falls.

I wonder what you dream, what landscape, the quality of light. Do you bring me your prey and drop it at my feet? Or do you mistake me for a white goat you spot and chase, your snout close to the ground, following the scent, hungry for my sinewy flesh and salted blood?

I wake to you from a dream of you. I think of the work it takes to go on breathing. How I am trying to stay alive. So I can go on trying to keep you alive. And my father alive. Though he was quick to agree to leave me here. Too quick, perhaps.

The day my father delivered me to you, I was impressed by the splendid table you had set for us, by your library, the harpsichord, the well-appointed rooms of my apartment in a section of the palace that is still habitable. I was struck by your kindness, Beast—the looking glass, these dressing gowns, the paisley shawl with fringe—little amenities you were able to provide despite the war, even at a time when supply lines were cut for weeks.

The blue light along the edge of the window drape has not

widened in all this time lying here. When I first woke, I thought it must be dawn. But the light comes from another source: the full moon.

As a girl, I used to sing myself to sleep. Now I think the lyric to myself, deep inside myself, "White coral bells upon a slender stalk / Lilies of the valley deck my garden walk." I join myself on the second phrase, silently voicing the words to make the first round. And when it's time for the fourth and fifth voices to come in, they do, each from a different part of myself, until I hear the whole song in the purest voices, more beautiful than when we sang it as girls at the convent school.

Angelic. As if angels themselves were singing round my head.

You shift your weight suddenly. You grunt. You move off my body. And I'm careful to protect my face from your sharp tusk.

My lovely, lovely face.

"Oh how I wish that you could hear them ring / But that will happen only."

I cannot for the life of me recall that last line. The words I fill in do not fit the present circumstance. Nor could they bring about the kind of miracle it would take.

"That will happen only when . . ."

We learned it at the convent, so perhaps it had something to do with Mary, Holy Mary, Mother of God.

"Oh how I wish that you could hear them ring / But that will happen only when . . ."

The angels sing. Of course. The angels. Not the Holy Mother. The angels. And not the fine lady in my dreams who assures me the virtue of giving up my life to save my father is its own reward.

Now a fat line of white light pushes out around the window drapes. I must have dozed off. You are no longer atop or beside me. I raise my arms straight up and let them fall. I kick my feet under the covers. I move my head from side to side. I can breathe.

My hand touches a patch of dried blood. Flecks of dried blood cover the sheets. They won't be brushed away. I'll have to take the sheets down to the river again and wash them, then lay them out in the sun to whiten. It won't get the stain out, but I hate the feeling of dried blood against my skin.

And it'll give me something to do.

There's a stream at the bottom of the garden that runs underneath the high walls. Sometimes when I rinse out the bedclothes, a dull brown tints the water, as if the stones were full of iron ore. And I wonder what the soldiers think on the other side of the wall, when the stream clouds. Or if they notice or recognize its origin as blood. And wonder if it's mine. Surely soldiers make jokes about that. About women bleeding.

By rights this ought to be my favorite time of day. I'm on my own. I can move about the palace as I choose—in the parts that are not off limits to me. I read. I play the harpsichord. I garden. But I'm lonely. And there is something menacing in this solitude, for I hear things I cannot see. Things I only half understand. Words from a language I shall never master.

But I know I am safe. Or that is something I have to believe. That I am safe. That the sound of the terrible machine that flies with its iron blades slicing the air above this tower belongs to us, not them. Ah. See? Not yet a full twelve months here, and I'm one of you. A being of indeterminate species, unspecified allegiance.

All I know is that I'm here, there is a war. All I know is that I'm at the mercy of a beast because my father cut a rose for me in the wrong forest. All I know is that I must stay here or my father will die. And I know other things. That my vain sisters were eager to see me go. That the care and attention and finery the Beast lavishes upon me serve one purpose—to exact from me the thing I cannot give: a promise of marriage.

Even the Bishop has been here to urge me. Imagine! The

Bishop! And when I reminded him of the vast number of martyred women in Church history, he scoffed. He called me vain. Impertinent. "They," he said, "were virgins." "You," he said, "are not." And he has a point. I am, at least not in the medical sense, any longer a virgin. But I do not *love* the Beast. I cannot. The Bishop scowls. He calls me proud. "What can you," he says, "a mere girl, know about love?"

I stood up. I shouted. Was it not enough that I was willing to sacrifice my life to save my father? What was it for, if not for love? And here, now, though I am subjected to humiliation upon humiliation, I submit, to keep this beast alive, for I cannot stand to see even him suffer. To marry him would be to lie to him. It would break his heart. So I refuse.

The Bishop rises. He makes the sign of the cross in the air before my face and leaves.

Lying, ignorant coward.

Each time he visits, I want to accuse him—of what, I still don't know, there must be something—and yet I hold my tongue.

Sometimes in the looking glass I see my father weep for missing me. Sometimes I see dark forms moving in the woods with bayonets. Sometimes I see circles of light and the fluttering of wings. And then, there is that fine lady who comes to me in dreams.

I hear voices. I have visions. There is no one to tell.

Now you are in the room with me again. You sniff along the mop board. You stop at every window to look out. You are startled by the sound of gunfire. As if you did not trust your own troops to protect us from whoever it is approaching from the woods farther down the mountain.

You are on edge, so agitated I cannot concentrate on the Bach Three Part Invention I'm trying to learn.

I can only guess your worry is about the war and how it's going, but I wonder if it might not be . . . something in you, battering the inside of your chest, trying to get out, something you want to show me but don't know how.

I can't keep my mind on what I'm doing. You vex me. You suck my attention from me. You steal my thoughts. As if it weren't enough to hold me hostage here, to own my body. I must also imagine what you think. Invent it for you. Speak it. Wait for your expression, the noises you make, interpret them.

That I must suffer this. And to what purpose?

You keep me fed and clothed. Housed in the part of a devastated castle that still stands. You keep me far away from a war raging in the cities.

I have reclaimed the ruined gardens. We have fresh lettuce, endives, tomatoes, turnips, leeks, pumpkins. Slowly, magically, the formal flower beds revive. And the rose, Beast, your pride, honor and emblem, the rose my father picked that sowed my doom. They are fine and huge and fragrant. The cool mountain air invigorates the bloom, refreshes the petals, and they hold on and on. They bloom and bloom again, despite the sudden snows. Already in one year we've had three separate growing seasons. The soil seems enchanted. At first, I struggled as though I were reinventing agriculture. For I knew nothing. And there was no one here to ask. Then the miracle. Once I'd cleared the plot of weed and rubble, I transplanted roots and cuttings from unknown stalks, put them all in rows, and there they were: carrots, aubergines, potatoes, acorn squash.

I've come to love the land.

It's the loneliness I mind. Trying to read your thoughts. Trying to give you comfort when you lay your great head in my lap. The loneliness of my own compassion. I often feel I can no longer endure not having anyone to answer me in my own language, a language I can share with other human beings.

For all your virtues, Beast, you are not human.

Despite your courage and decisiveness as a general or colonel or president, whatever you are. Despite your care for me and your loyal protection, the love you show. Even despite the indications you love music when you lie quietly as I play and do not scratch or lick yourself or bite your fleas.

You are not human.

I have voices. I see visions. There is no one here to tell.

I wake to you from a dream of you. The work it takes to go on breathing. How I try to stay alive. So I can keep you alive. And my father alive.

But that's not what troubles me. Remember: I was ready to die from the beginning. It's the apparent purposelessness. That it seems to have no meaning. It's what I hadn't planned on, couldn't have known. To keep myself alive, so that Fate can grind me to a nub when She sees fit.

In one dream, my face hardens. My cheeks turn to porcelain. The tip of my nose freezes. I am turning to stone, despite my virtue, despite my sacrifice.

Not that I'm bitter. It's that I have these dreams. You must understand. But of course you don't, you can't. Even awake, you are dumb, insensible. All you do is growl and drool as you trot about the palace, sniffing at the drapery and the doors.

Sometimes I think we are both merely biding our time, waiting to be annihilated by our own boredom, or the corrosive damp that will one day pull the remaining walls down, or the troops we hear moving, moving through the wood, up and down the mountain, night after night. The other troops. Or your own, Beast.

You'd never harm me on purpose. It's the accidents I've got to watch out for.

In another dream, I see you in a field. Your limbs, the strong flanks pumping, running. You leap and turn. I am stunned by your beauty. I wake gasping for breath.

Where does it go, the love I feel for you then, the awe that fills me, the joy that quickens my blood? Where does it go, the power in you I admire in an open field when it is away from me? What does it become when you lie atop me, wheezing and grunting, fucking, fucking?

Again and again, I wake to you from a dream of you. Gasping for breath. The work it takes to go on breathing. The work it takes to stay alive. To keep you alive. And my father alive.

I often think we are both waiting for annihilation. Some political shift. For the tanks to crumble the high wall and tear through the garden. Their tanks. Or yours.

More often than not, I suspect we've been abandoned by God. And then I see it again. At the bottom of the garden, a red-winged angel stands, holding something out towards me, an offering which looks suspiciously like a rose.

Dedicated to the memory of the Martyrs of Beijing
—also disappeared, June 4, 1989

Florence Wearnse

*W*hen the rock shattered the parlor window, jostled the glass globe resting on the sash, and flew past the lamp on the table, it hit Florence Wearnse's teacup, broke it clean from its handle, and sent it crashing against the wall not far from where her sister Hope stood straightening a portrait of their father, who, because of some terrible misunderstanding and through no fault of his own, was in prison, and who, had he been at home, would have been deeply insulted by the rock that had broken the window and left the teacup handle perched delicately between the thumb and forefinger of Florence's slender right hand as she leaned forward, with pursed lips, ready to sip the empty air, while Hope charged toward the front door. She did not take it lightly, this insult to her father's honor, the boys hollering, "Kraut Face! Sauer Kraut! Traitor!" But by the time she had reached the top step of the veranda, the boys had fled more than a block down the street that had, up until the week before, been called Berlin, but which had been renamed Pershing by the city fathers, who, in a ceremony that was as long and as loud as it was patriotic, had warned St. Louisans of German descent who might still harbor some misguided sympathy for Kaiser Wilhelm to show their love of America in everything they did, so that when Hope hiked up her skirts to light out after the boys, she thought better of it, shook her fist at them instead, and came back into the parlor, grumbling, to find Florence on her knees, picking up the broken bits of teacup.

As she mopped the tea with a damp cloth, Florence thought, Outbursts such as these make people think Hope is difficult and headstrong, and she wished her sister were less demonstrative about her emotion. It was often quite unsettling, and a curious expression, demonstrative, thought Florence, picturing a small beast curled at the center of the word, waiting to spring, and, once having leapt, growing to several times its original size, changing shape as it grew, until she saw her sister as a wrathful dragon covered over with green scales, her tail curling this way and that as she lumbered down the street after the boys, breathing great pointed lengths of yellow flame. But Florence was interrupted by Hope's voice, "Leave that for the maid; it's what she's paid for," which is what their father would have said had he been there, what he did say, in fact, after he himself dove through the closed parlor window, shattering the glass, jarring the globe, toppling the lamp, breaking the table, drunk, bellowing, laughing, home from World War I, a story that got told over and over again, long after Hope's children had grown and married real Americans with English names like Thompson, Mansfield, and Jones, so that there was no question of their allegiance during World War II and the twenty-three years Florence lived afterwards, her whole life a spinster, though no one could quite understand why—she had the best posture of any woman in St. Louis and an amiable disposition—and so people concluded that she'd had her heart broken, that her father had caught her spooning on the veranda with an unsuitable suitor, or that the suitor, having had too much to drink in a beer garden one night, went out wandering along the river bank, fell in, and was drowned before he even had a chance to ask Florence for her hand.

So people looked at Florence a little sadly because no one had wanted her, and because, as Hope was fond of saying during the years of the Great Depression, Florence was one of the Army of the Unenjoyed, none of which bothered Florence, who was perfectly suited to the life she was living, first with her mother, and then with Hope and her children, all of whom would run into the big kitchen after school and call for their Aunt Florence instead of their mother because Florence was more attentive to their child ambitions and joys and worries. Especially when they were young, the children found Florence to be full of esoteric knowledge, so adept at Chinese checkers that they thought she must have gone all the way to China to learn how to play, and imagined her adjusting her hatpin as she stepped out of the rickshaw, climbed the stairs to the pagoda, and bowed to the Chinaman with a Fu Manchu who wore long silk robes embroidered with suns, dragons, shooting stars, moons, and, without flinching, she'd say in Chinese, "Good afternoon, Professor Wong, how are you today?" and he'd say, "Very well, thank you, Miss Wearnse, shall we begin?" and they would walk through the open courtyard, past a fountain full of lotus blossoms, to the room where he taught her all he knew about Chinese checkers, which is why she won every time they played, and which seemed the source of her power, until years later they realized they loved her because she listened to them with a deeper attention than she gave to all the quiet, clean-living bachelors and widowers Hope arranged to have call on Sunday afternoons, friends of her husband, men who were usually no more interested in being married than Florence was.

But she would smile nevertheless, and pour tea, and listen to one talk about his trade journals, another about the price of lumber, the war, President Wilson, or the streetcar wreck last Wednesday, as he fumbled with the delicate teacakes and dabbed the corner of his mouth with a white linen napkin before he rose, said what a pleasant time he'd had, excused himself, and left Florence to wipe up the crumbs, wash the cups, and get back to her tiny maid's room at the back of the house, where she could be alone with a volume of Thoreau or Mary Baker Eddy, or her own thoughts, which she preferred to those of others. So much so that she finally went deaf to escape the listening, so tired had she grown of stocks and bonds, whooping cough, motor cars, weddings, the Kentucky Derby, nursemaids, Europe, football, draperies, scarlet fever, President Roosevelt, the World Series, measles, and the whole litany of troubles other women brought to her, until Christmas of 1957, when Florence decided to be deaf, and sat watching everybody rock back and forth, slapping their knees at some joke she had not heard, for she would never hear again, and she was so relieved that she stretched her mouth into a thin, colorless smile which remained a long time after everyone had lit up a Lucky Strike, taken a sip of bourbon, and returned to talking about some serious business of life.

Then Florence, full of this new blessing of silence, began to giggle, her shoulders quivering a bit, and to laugh out loud for no reason that was apparent to the others, which made them think what they had suspected for some time now, that she was in the years of her decline, and Hope stopped for a moment, the only moment in her life she felt (but how could it be true?) that she had robbed Florence of something, somehow, a life of her own perhaps, and she thought of her sister, years younger, a beautiful woman with a straight back, striding down Delmar Boulevard with a satchel of music under her arm, on her way to give a mandolin lesson, Florence seated on a shield-back chair in the parlor of fine people who had done very well for themselves (now she remembered), railroad people who'd made a fortune, and whose front parlor made Florence look plain and dowdy and more than a little silly (she had never learned to primp, never thought about making herself pretty; she simply hadn't tried), listening to her student's finger exercise, nodding, counting to herself, one and two, and "not so stiff, and yes that's better," pointing to the music, showing the child the chords, playing them herself as she hummed along (a fool! oblivious to public opinion).

And then Hope knew it was Florence who had robbed *her* of something, was robbing her of something as she sat there, giggling at nothing, beyond her, beyond all the rest of them now, so that Hope wanted to rise up out of her chair, walk across the room, and slap Florence's face to bring her back, to reclaim her, the last woman alive who remembered their girlhood together, and Hope knew she had resented it all along, her sister's privacy, her spinsterly distance, the years she had shared with her friend Edwina, who'd been Hope's friend first, a girl they'd grown up with, but who, as courting, marriage, babies, and society took more and more of Hope's time, had grown closer to Florence, for they were both spinsters and sat for hours at the kitchen table, drinking tea together, watching the light change at the window as if there were nothing better to do in the late afternoon than to arrange flowers, share books, perceptions, secrets, which excluded her, so that now, more than anything else in the world, she wanted Florence back, wanted Edwina back, wanted to stay in the kitchen filled with their voices and their laughter without being pulled away to the children, the men, in other parts of the house, the luncheon appointments in other parts of the city, and it pained her now to think that Florence wouldn't think about her much after she died, which, as it turned out, was true.

Not that Florence bore her sister any malice, she was incapable of that, but, some years after Hope's death, on what was to be Florence's own last day on earth, she rose in the morning, put the kettle on to boil, stood at the grimy window in her small apartment on Delmar, fingered the leaf of a philodendron, touched the soil to see if it needed water, picked up the glass globe which rested on the window sash, held it up to the light, and, looking through it, watched people outside stop at the vegetable stand, the drugstore, the butcher, watched a bus pull up, and, though her friend had been dead for over a year, Florence was sure she saw Edwina get off the bus and stop at the flower shop across the street— the whole vision curled in the glass globe: street, vegetable stand, bus, tree, shops, sky, Edwina with an arm full of daisies . . . a trick of light so delicate that Florence dared not breathe.

At Home
with the Pelletiers

*H*oward was just getting used to the idea that his older brother was gone forever, and that he might at last have the bedroom they had always shared to himself. But here was Walter back in St. Louis again, this time from boot camp in California, a United States Marine. "I have been trained to kill," he announced, and when their mother smiled and said how proud she was of him, Walter grinned and squinted at her and told them about a man, a leatherneck home on leave who, when he was suddenly and carelessly woken up, had jumped out of bed and torn his mother's throat right out of her neck in one gesture. Walter jabbed his right hand into the air, made a fist, twisted it, and drew it back into his shoulder, crying, "Aaaiiiii . . . AH." Walter glanced at their mother from time to time as he was telling the story to see if she took his meaning. She glared back at him, still smiling, but in such a way that Howard knew she'd go right on waking them both up at seven o'clock, just the way she always did.

And then Howard noticed she cocked her head and looked perplexed, as if she were thinking that "Aaaiiiii . . . AH" did not sound to her like an American war cry; it sounded Japanese, and as she recollected, the Japanese had been the enemy in the last war, and so it looked to Howard like she was beginning to wonder just whose side Walter was on. And she looked sad that Walter was now too strong for her to whip him with the strap that still hung behind the pantry door.

Howard pushed the gas pedal down with his right foot, but nothing happened. The car rolled through the intersection and came to a stop just short of the parking lot next to Skruggs, Vandervorts & Barney. He turned the key in the ignition and pumped the gas, but the car wouldn't start up again. Walter was going to be pissed off. He said if he'd been around, he would never have let their mother buy it in the first place. He said she had been robbed blind.

A man behind him honked the horn, so Howard waved him around. He was afraid to get out of the car. He hadn't had his license for even two weeks yet, and he didn't want to draw attention to himself. He didn't know anything about how a car worked, outside the fact that when you turned the key and stepped on the gas pedal it was supposed to go. He knew that cars ran out of gas, but the needle was almost at full, which might mean the gas gauge was broken. Or that the car was flooded.

He wasn't real sure what it meant for a car to be flooded. It had something to do with there being too much gas, and you were in danger of doing it if you pressed the gas pedal down too hard or too often when you were starting the car. "Go easy," Walter had told him, "don't flood the engine." And Howard pictured a pool of gasoline rising up, submerging the motor.

Walter had been driving for five years already and knew all about how cars worked. He knew what was wrong with them when they didn't run and how to change a flat tire. He had explained to Howard again and again what a carburetor was and how rods and cylinders and spark plugs all worked together to make a car run.

There was a tap on the window. Howard jumped. He rolled the window down, and a policeman leaned over to ask what the problem was.

"I must have flooded the engine," said Howard.

"Well," said the policeman, "you'll have to get it off the street. I can't have you holding up rush hour traffic."

"But it won't go," said Howard.

"Then you'll have to get out and push it, won't you?" said the officer.

Howard knew that wouldn't work. If he got out and pushed, who would steer? And even if he'd been the right size for his age and lifted weights, he couldn't push a 1955 Buick Century out of the way all by himself.

"Put it in neutral," said the officer.

"Neutral," Howard repeated to himself. He moved the lever on the steering column until the red metal triangle reached the letter *N*. Then he waited.

A man from the sidewalk and the officer's partner came over to help push.

"Steer into the parking lot," shouted the policeman.

Howard bunched his eyebrows together and stared straight ahead. He pushed his right cheek out with his tongue and strained forward, waiting for the car to move, which it did, with a jerk at first, and then more smoothly. He pulled on the steering wheel hard, to the right, and the car started up the slight incline that led into the parking lot.

"What do you mean, stopped?" his mother said over the phone.

"I don't know. It just stopped," said Howard. He was in a phone booth near the gift wrapping department on the third floor of

Vandervort's. "I can't get it started up again. I thought I'd flooded the engine, so I waited a while, but it still won't start."

"Did you look under the hood?"

Howard knew he should have done this. It's what most sixteen-year-old boys would do, but most sixteen-year-old boys at least knew how to make it look like they understood what they were doing. Howard didn't. If he had opened up the hood, he'd have stood there, gaping, with the names of parts like crankcase, camshaft, and alternator jangling around in his head.

"I don't know what any of it means, Mom."

He knew his mother felt he ought to know. He also knew she didn't know any more about cars than he did. She said she'd call Dick Dunham's garage, and maybe he could send over one of his boys with the tow truck.

Howard could hear Walter's voice in the background.

"Hold the line a second," his mother said. "I can't talk to two people at once—Howard? Your brother says to ask you if the radio was on. He says if the radio works, the battery's still good. He says go back and turn on the radio and see."

"OK," said Howard, "but here's the thing. The thing is, it's almost five o'clock and the store's going to close. The parking lot attendant says he puts the chain up around five-thirty most evenings, so I guess we've kind of got to get the car out of there pretty soon, wouldn't you say?"

"I most certainly would," said his mother. "I'll go ahead and call Dick Dunham's and have him send one of the boys right over. He can give you a lift home if he can't get the car started."

Howard wished this weren't happening. He was mortified. When Dick Dunham's boy came, he would ask Howard what the trouble was, and Howard wouldn't be able to tell him. He was afraid Dick Dunham's boy would give him a disgusted look and shake his head. Dick Dunham's boys weren't much older than Howard, but they were tall and muscular, with black hair already grown on their forearms, and oil and black grit under their fingernails. They smelled like gasoline. It was a smell Howard found so pleasant that he had once told Walter, "You know, I don't think it would be so bad to die in the gas chamber. If I was on Death Row, and they gave me a choice, I'd pick the gas chamber any day. I kind of like the smell of gas."

Walter shook his head and set his jaw and squinted his eyes, as though he couldn't believe anybody human could be so entirely ignorant. "It's not the same kind of gas," he said. "It's a little pellet of *poison* gas. They drop it in acid to eat away the plastic capsule. It hisses and smells terrible."

"So you figure the electric chair would be quicker?" Howard said.

"Oh yeah, much quicker," said Walter. "The trouble is, sometimes they don't give you enough juice the first time, so you sit there and twitch until they give you another jolt strong enough to do the job."

Howard thought that didn't sound so bad. He pictured a man sitting in a chair, his arms and legs in straps, a little metal band around his head. He pictured the man smiling to himself, peaceful, like his mother when she fell asleep in a living room chair. Except she snored and ground her teeth, and he knew dead people didn't do that.

But he had the wrong picture. Walter explained that the electrocuted jerked and spasmed before they died. They got fried all over, and their skin turned black and crusty and smelled burnt, which made Howard prefer the gas chamber again, even if it was slower. He went back to imagining that the gas smelled like gasoline, at least a little.

What did Walter know, anyway?

Howard heard the kitchen door slam. His mother and Walter were arguing about the Buick again. Dick Dunham's boy had gotten it started, and Dick Dunham himself had fixed it enough to drive it back, but now it wouldn't start again, and Walter was pitching a fit. "If I had been here, I'd have never let you *buy* the goddamned thing. I tell you, they robbed you *blind*. Not only does it not run right, but some asshole painted it *powder blue,* for chrissake."

"Walter, I've warned you about using that kind of language in my house. Now that'll do. I won't have it."

Walter said she was putting Howard's life in danger by letting him drive it. He said it might break down anywhere and cause a pile-up on the highway. He said if she weren't so goddamned cheap she'd have bought a decent secondhand car for Howard to drive. "And what am *I* supposed to do?" he shrieked. "How can I find myself a job without reliable transportation? How do you expect me to get around? Call a helicopter?"

Howard sat very still on his desk chair in the bedroom upstairs. He knew somehow that he was the cause of this ruckus. He wished he had never learned to drive. In fact, if he had never turned sixteen, his mother would never have bought the car. "A lemon," Walter called it, "a fucking powder-blue lemon." And if the Vietnam War had never started, Walter might never have joined the Marine Corps Reserves and come back from boot camp this way. He might still be going to the University of Missouri at Columbia, like he did before all this happened.

The kitchen door slammed again. His mother yelled, "Leave Howard alone. He's trying to study." He heard Walter leap up the stairs three at a time. The door opened. Howard turned and stared at his brother, who was breathing hard and grinning.

"Come on," said Walter, "I want you to see something."

Howard got up and followed his brother downstairs. He could hear his mother down in the basement, kicking the washing machine and pounding the top of it with her fists. He stopped for a second at the basement door, but Walter turned around and said, "Come on."

When they reached the car, Walter unscrewed the gas cap, put it on the roof, and started feeding string down into the gas tank. Howard hung back a little. He looked over his shoulder to see if the next-door neighbors were watching. He knew better than to try and talk Walter out of this, but he didn't want to have anything to do with it.

By the time Walter had lit the match, their mother was struggling to get into the passenger side. She didn't say a word, and once she had locked all the doors, she put both hands on the steering wheel and looked straight forward. Walter looked like he was going to go right ahead and put the match to the string anyway, but he stopped. He walked up to the window, leaned over so that his face was next to the glass, and, holding the match between his thumb and forefinger, blew out the flame.

Their mother gave the handle a crank and the window slid down about three quarters of an inch. She leaned up into the open space without first looking at Walter. She twisted her mouth, as though she were getting ready to say something. Then she cut him a scared, angry look and said, "Walter Pelletier, you be out of my house by six o'clock this evening or I'm calling the police."

She took hold of the steering wheel again with both hands, as if the car were going to start up on its own and she were going to drive it slowly and deliberately straight ahead, through the back wall of the garage, through the fence behind it, on into the Kennedys' back field, and into the woods beyond that. Howard pictured the hole in the back of the garage, the broken rails of the fence, the mud ruts in the Kennedys' field, as the car plowed through the woods, straight for the new shopping center at the other side of it. He could just see his mother pull into a parking space, with branches all over the hood and roof, like camouflage.

"She won't call the police," said Walter. "She wouldn't dare." He winked so as to reassure Howard. "Men in uniform share a bond. If a police officer did come here, he'd find a United States Marine in charge. And who knows? I might be the one to call the police . . . to have me some help getting this old lady into an insane asylum."

They sat on the couch in front of the television set on the sun porch. Walter was drinking a cold beer. Howard had just come home from school and dropped his books down between them. Walter wore pale blue boxer shorts and a white V-neck T-shirt. His arms were sunburned and his face was sunburned, but the rest of his body was pale—bleached, as if the true color had been drained out of the flesh—because his uniform in boot camp had covered him up mostly.

In high school, Walter had run on the relay team and played varsity basketball. He was tough and fast and graceful. On Saturday mornings in the fall, Howard had learned to get up without making any noise so Walter could sleep late, and by ten o'clock the house would be filled with the smell of broiling steak for Walter's breakfast. He needed plenty of lean, red meat before each football game he played in, and one year they had almost won the State Championship.

In those days, Walter had put Howard on a rigorous program of jumping jacks, push-ups, chin-ups. He would hold Howard's feet and count as Howard struggled to sit up and touch his right elbow to his left knee, and his left elbow to his right knee, fifteen, sixteen, . . . ("Come on Howie, just one more.") . . . seventeen times until he could not sit up anymore. But after two whole weeks of daily exercise, his biceps were no thicker and his chest measured the same as it had before. His eleven-year-old body had failed to transform itself. He was sore and could hardly move, so he gave up and took to exercising sporadically, in a kind of fury, when Walter wasn't around to supervise.

The truth was, Howard's feeling about his brother's body had grown so deep and painful he could not even give it a name.

On his first night home from boot camp, when they were alone together getting ready for bed, Walter stripped to his boxer shorts to show his new body to Howard. Pointing to the ridges over his belly, he told Howard to punch it as hard as he could. "Come on," he said, "it won't hurt me." With his new body, Walter looked something like the weight lifters pictured in the back of comic books, but there was a difference. Walter wasn't all hunched over the way they were. Even so, he had gained fifteen pounds, and he looked bigger, as if the Marines had pumped him up with fluid or air, but when he punched his brother's stomach, Howard knew it wasn't fluid or air; it was more like cement.

Walter had always warned him against the bodybuilding courses they advertised in comic books. He said unsupervised weight lifting could ruin you as an athlete. But here he was back from the Marines, looking like he did. Walter said it was because of the miles and miles of marching and all of the endurance tests he was put to, but Howard wondered for a minute if it hadn't ruined him as an athlete after all.

On TV, Jane Fonda was telling the talk show host what she thought about the war in Vietnam, and the housewives in the studio audience were standing up to ask her why she didn't just move to Russia or go over there and live in Hanoi if she felt that way.

Every once in a while, their mother would walk in front of

them on her way to dust something at the opposite end of the sun porch. She stopped once, looking at the TV, and said, "Imagine that. Henry Fonda's own daughter. I bet she's breaking his heart." Walter snorted. They still weren't speaking. Each time his mother walked in front of him and blocked his view of the TV set, he leaned to his right or to his left and then shot back upright as soon as she passed, so he wouldn't miss anything.

Walter looked upset. He had always liked Jane Fonda, especially in that movie *Barbarella,* and he was shocked that she sympathized with the Communists. "Even so," he said, "if the men in my division were to tie her down and gang-bang her, I'd skip my turn out of respect."

It made Howard sick when Walter said stuff like that. Howard liked Jane Fonda, and he hadn't even seen *Barbarella.* He liked it that she could go on national television and tell everybody exactly what she thought of the war, and he agreed with her, though he'd never let on. Not in this family. But even though Howard felt sick when his brother talked like that, he was desperate for information about sex, and as repulsive as gang-banging sounded to Howard, he had to know if this was one day going to be expected of him.

Walter was full of terrifying stories about boot camp. Once, he and a few of his buddies had gone into the town. His buddies had all found themselves girls, but Walter hadn't. Finally they went to a bar and Walter struck up a conversation with a blonde-haired woman who was a full head taller than he was, with a square jaw and a big nose. Walter said he felt sorry for her and he thought he was giving her a break. Besides, he said, she had nice legs, and he was drunk by then anyway, so he kept saying over and over, "I'm a leg man. Yes sirree, that's what I am—a leg man."

Then they went and parked somewhere, and he started to make out with the girl in the backseat. Everything went fine for a while.

She was a good kisser. When he started feeling her up outside her dress, one of her breasts shifted to her shoulder, which meant she was wearing falsies, but he didn't hold that against her. A girl did whatever she had to do to look appealing to a man, and a man ought to do whatever he could to appreciate her effort. But when he put his hand down her pants, he said he let out a cry as if something had bit him. "Cause you know what I found in her panties?"

Howard shook his head.

"A dick and balls. She had a dick and balls the same as you and me."

Howard's mouth dropped open, and he shut it so quick his teeth banged together. He couldn't imagine what kind of woman would have a dick and balls. He figured she must have escaped from a freak show like the Royal American Circus.

"She was a man, Howie. A man dressed up like a woman."

Howard couldn't imagine this either.

"So I hauled him out of the car, but I didn't let the others know what happened, see? I made like we were going into the woods to fuck, and when we were far enough away, I kicked his butt and he ran off." Walter shook his head. "Shit," he said.

He told other stories too. One was about a race riot. Another was about a new recruit who slit his wrists with a bayonet. The drill sergeant said it was just so as to get sent home, so he sat the guy in a chair and made all the others stand around to watch as he cried and hung his arms down at his side and bled all over the floor. Walter said that was nothing; one man had hung himself in the shower room. And then he told about the movie they'd seen about VD and how to avoid catching it, and what to do if for any reason you should happen to get it. Howard was beginning to think some of the stories were tall tales, but there was something so urgent and insistent in his brother's voice when he told them that Howard couldn't help but listen to how Marines sliced the ears and genitals off the Viet Cong and wore them around their necks, until the stories about sex and the stories about war atrocities became hard to distinguish one from the other.

Their mother called to Howard from the basement door. She wanted him to come help her move the washing machine back into place. It would get to vibrating and shaking so violently that it walked across the floor until it pulled its own plug out of the wall. Howard shouted out, "Be right there," and he got up from the couch to go. Walter shot him a murderous look which said, WHOSE SIDE ARE YOU ON?

Howard shrugged and went downstairs to help his mother.

His mother stood to the left of the washing machine, and Howard took his usual position on the right. He put his hands flat on the front and leaned his shoulder down into them. He gave the machine a shove that moved it back a bit and angled it to the right. His mother did the same, which moved her end back in line with Howard's. They continued this way, first Howard and then his mother, until the machine was almost flush against the wall again and his mother could plug it back in. Once the machine was running, she lit a cigarette and asked, "Has your brother started packing?"

Howard knew what she wanted to hear, but lying would only make things worse because she'd assume that a solution was at hand, and it wasn't.

"Not that I've seen," he said.

"Howard," she said, "you've got to talk to him."

"Mom. If he's not going to listen to you, what makes you think he's going to listen to me?"

"You're his brother, Howard."

Howard opened his mouth to respond, but there was something so powerful and complicated beginning to work in his mind that he shut it again and walked back upstairs.

His mother sat at the head of the table. Howard sat to her right. The chair on her left was empty, though a place was set.

"Go call your brother."

"I already did."

"Well do it again. Everything's getting cold."

Howard went to the foot of the stairs and hollered up to his brother that supper was ready. Then he came back and sat down. His mother smiled, shook her napkin, and put it on her lap. She stabbed a chicken leg and dropped it on a plate next to a large pile of lima beans and four round slices of beets. She was about to stab a breast when Howard said no thank you. He wasn't hungry. "Nonsense," said his mother as she lifted the breast and gave it a shake so that it fell onto the plate next to the leg. "You're right in the middle of a growth spurt. Starving yourself won't do. It just won't do."

Walter marched into the dining room without a word, kicked his right leg up over the back of his chair, and sat down. He wore his black boots and Marine-issue camouflage pants and shirt with a camouflage cap on his head. He set a small kit of field eating utensils on the table and winked at Howard. When he reached over to grab himself a piece of fried chicken, his mother jabbed his hand with her fork. He drew his injured hand back and put it in his mouth. "What the hell was that for?" he cried.

His mother turned to Howard and asked him to tell his brother that civilians do not grab for food with their hands at the supper table; they wait until they are served. "And would you mind asking him to please take off his hat while he's at the table? Thank you, Howard."

Howard looked at Walter, asking him with his eyes to cooperate, so he wouldn't have to repeat. Howard had an algebra test first thing the next morning, and he was beginning to feel sick to his stomach.

Walter took the plate that his mother handed him. He picked up a chicken leg. "I'm a leg man," he said. "Yes sirree, that's what I am—a leg man." He grinned at Howard and took a bite out of the drumstick. Howard looked down at his own plate.

"Howard," said their mother, "would you ask your brother to please not eat his chicken with his fingers?"

"Since when is it against the law to eat fried chicken with your fingers? We always used to eat it that way."

Their mother smiled at Howard and said, "First, tell him not to talk with his mouth full. Then tell him that's just the way it is under my roof these days, and if he doesn't like it, he can jolly well go elsewhere."

Walter glared at his mother and went right on eating with his fingers—not just the chicken, but the beans and beets too. Their mother smiled and commenced having a nice, friendly conversation with Howard about school and the upcoming algebra test and her friends' daughters who were in his class. Howard didn't say much. He had grown sullen. That's what his mother called it, but he was really just trying not to throw up, and he avoided Walter's glance for fear his mother would catch him winking or nodding at him and think it signaled some secret collusion Howard wanted nothing to do with.

In fact, Howard had about decided he wanted nothing to do with this family at all. Almost the only thing that made him feel good anymore was to think what it would be like to catch a bus to Chicago or New York City. And even then, he had to stick to what the view was like from the bus window, because each time he pictured a bus station he saw sad and dirty people standing around looking mean and lost, and each time he pictured beyond that, once he'd arrived in Chicago or New York, all he could see was himself walking down the street, with the collar of his coat turned up, and lugging a suitcase, and being followed by a tall, blonde-haired woman with a square jaw. Or he saw himself sitting on a narrow bed in a rented room, listening to other people in the rooming house argue or cough or call out to each other. Besides, he didn't have but $16, which wasn't enough to get him anywhere, even if he knew how to get to the bus station downtown, which he didn't, and it wasn't like he could just hop in the old Buick and drive off; it was not a reliable automobile.

So Howard had pretty much decided to stick it out in his mother's house until he went off to college. Because if he didn't go to college, he'd get drafted, and if he got drafted, he might end up acting like Walter was acting right now. (He looked over to Walter and found him chewing rhythmically, bobbing his head up and down and blinking like a red-assed circus monkey.) Or worse. If boot camp was as bad as Walter said it was, what was Vietnam like? And how did people act when they got back . . . if they ever did come back?

Just last week, he heard at school that Sandy Podmaninsky had been killed over there, and they were sending him home in a box. At first, Howard pictured a long, white cardboard box, the kind that gladiolas came in, only larger. And it had taken him a minute to picture a coffin like the ones they showed on TV in rows and rows, lined up on some runway, all of them alike and made of pine . . . and now Sandy Podmaninsky was in one of them. Howard didn't mention it, not just because Sandy and Walter had been on the same relay team in high school, but because he was afraid Walter would grab onto this and work it around in his mind and think: that could be me someday.

And Walter kept reminding them. Any day, he said, he could be called into active service and sent overseas, but he'd been saying that for eight months now and the order still had not come.

Leaning against one wall of their bedroom closet was a shotgun Walter used when he was Howard's age to shoot squirrels. The gun hadn't been used in years and was wrapped in a brown felt cloth. The box of shells still lay in Walter's top drawer. They were made of red cardboard fashioned into long tubes with a brass base. The box was to the right of Walter's underwear and socks and in front of his box of rubbers. Years ago, he bought a box of twenty individually wrapped Trojans, and there was only one missing. That was the one Walter kept in his wallet. Howard checked from time to time to make sure. He figured Walter bought the rubbers he used day to day at the drugstore or the gas station or the barbershop. He figured the box in the dresser drawer was just for emergency reserve, but every once in a while Howard found himself wondering if Walter might not still be a virgin.

Howard was careful about going through his brother's things. Walter had forbidden him to touch anything of his unless he was there himself. That had always been the rule, and he had reminded Howard of it before he'd gone off to the state university. He'd made three exceptions. Howard could wear his neckties if he was careful not to spill food on them. He could play with the basketball if he made sure there was always just the right amount of air in it. And he could play the conga drum if he made sure his hands were spotless.

Walter hadn't mentioned anything about the shotgun because Howard had never shown any interest in hunting squirrels.

At the moment, Walter was in the shower and Howard was getting disgusted with the algebra problem he'd been staring at for the last quarter of an hour. He got up from his desk and went over to Walter's side of the room and picked up one of the stones Walter brought back with him from the Arizona desert. He wondered where Walter had found it and tried to picture what had been lying around it. He imagined the warmth it had absorbed from the sun and held the stone tight, trying to warm it again. He wondered about its power and the power it seemed to lend his brother, who'd traveled out West all those summers with a science teacher from the high school. He'd seen the Grand Canyon. He'd ridden horses. He'd slid down hard-packed snowbanks in the Teton Mountains in July while in St. Louis Howard had sweltered and sweated and tried to move slowly and sit still because the air was so thick and heavy.

Howard put the stone down and went back to his desk. He heard Walter turn the shower off. The bathroom door banged open right after that, and Howard thought the hot water had run out. Their mother was downstairs doing the supper dishes. Howard turned in his chair to suggest that Walter wait a half hour and try again, when Walter came flying through the open bedroom door. He was literally in midair, his legs spread in a leap, his mouth open, and out of it came some kind of wild and joyous cry that Howard took to be more of the jujitsu talk Walter had picked up in the Marines. Before his foot even touched the rug, Walter grabbed the towel from around his waist, balled it up, and threw it, hitting Howard right in the face.

"Cut it out, Walter. I'm trying to study."

Howard picked the towel up off the floor, threw it back at his brother, and turned to his algebra book. From downstairs came their mother's voice: "Howard? Is Walter bothering you? Tell him to quit now. You've got that test tomorrow."

Howard rolled his eyes and stuck out his tongue. Then he went to the bedroom door and hollered, "He's showing me some very important military strategies to use against the Viet Cong. He says we should all learn them, you too, Mom, because we have no way of knowing how this war is going to turn out. He says the government's not giving us all the right information. Not by a long shot. Why, those gooks might be hiding out in the Ozarks, or sneaking through the bushes along Route 40 right this very minute."

Their mother went back into the kitchen without bothering to answer. She turned on the garbage disposal and let it roar.

Walter hopped from one foot to the other and waved his arms. He shouted, "Aaaiiiii" and "OOOOOOOh" and "AH" and his penis wagged up and down. He leapt over to the conga drum, crouched down with it between his knees, and began to slap the animal skin with the three middle fingers of each hand. Then he put one elbow on the skin to change the sound.

Howard sat on his bed and watched. Walter jerked his head, motioning Howard to stand up. Howard turned and stared out the window. He was failing algebra. His only hope was to get an A on this next test, and he'd never get an A no matter how hard he studied. It was useless. All the letters and numbers and formulas just froze his mind, and the only way to be free of algebra forever was to graduate from high school, and the only way he was going to graduate from high school year after next was to pass algebra. The only way he was going to college was to graduate from high school, and so if he failed algebra, Howard was sure he'd be drafted and sent to Vietnam.

He wanted to take off his clothes and join his brother, have a turn at the drum while his brother danced, but he was afraid. He was ashamed of his body. It had betrayed him. It had not grown tall enough, become thick enough, or sprouted hair in the right patterns or places. And he almost always got an erection for no reason at all, so that sometimes in class he'd have to pretend he didn't have a dick to try to make it go away. He would sneak quick glances at his classmates and the older boys in the locker room gang shower at school. Their bodies—so many of them perfectly formed, beautifully proportioned, reddening under the hot water, glowing through the steam—their bodies and the ease, the off-handed way they seemed to live in them made Howard ashamed of his own. He would walk carefully on the slippery tile, with his shoulders slumped, turned away, turning in on himself, trying to hide his genitals with one hand without looking like he was doing so. He would twist the handle on the wall and stand for a mo-ment under a stream of cold water, without getting his hair wet because that only made his hair greasier than it was ordinarily. He would try not to watch the others soaping themselves casually as they talked and laughed. Soaping himself meant touching his body, and he couldn't do that, not in public, for he was never sure what it would do in response.

Just then, Walter grabbed Howard by the shoulders and pulled him up off the bed. Howard felt a hot, stinging electrical pulse shoot through his arms and chest and into his groin. This startled him so badly he shoved his hands up between his brother's arms, thrust his forearms out, and broke Walter's hold on him. Wal-ter took a step back and tilted his head to one side, grinning at Howard as if this were the beginning of a friendly wrestling match, but before Walter could do anything else, Howard put his head down and charged, hitting Walter in the stomach right below the rib cage, and drove him back across their room to his own side, landing him on his bed.

Walter wasn't stunned for long. He grabbed the front of Howard's shirt before Howard could even think to straighten up and run. Walter stood up and pulled Howard to his feet and toward him in one motion. Then he drew his right fist back and held Howard at a distance, ready to smash him in the face. Howard waited, almost as though he deserved it because in his brother's eyes, he now saw the most curious mixture of outrage, fear, and deep sadness he'd ever seen.

Howard closed his eyes. He felt the knot of fisted cloth loosen over his chest and heard Walter walk over and snatch the towel up from the floor. He felt Walter's presence drain from the room as he heard him close the bathroom door and turn on the shower.

Howard failed the algebra test. He didn't go right home after school that day. He felt like being alone for a while, so he hung out in the woods, smoking cigarettes. When he did go home, it was almost six o'clock, but there were no lights on in the house, even though it was already dark outside. He walked through the kitchen without turning on a light. It wasn't until he reached the stairs that he heard his mother's voice coming from outside his bedroom. It sounded soft and soothing and urgent. She hadn't even heard Howard come in.

He turned on the hall light, and once he was part way up the stairs he saw his mother sitting on a straight-back chair she'd pulled up to the open bedroom door. She'd brought up an ashtray from the kitchen and a bottle of Coca-Cola. Judging from the number of cigarette butts in the ashtray, she'd been sitting there quite a while. She was leaning over, her arms resting on her knees. Then she turned and reached for her Coca-Cola. The minute she saw Howard, she frowned and shook her head. She waved her hand at him to shoo him away.

Everything was so peculiar about the dark house and the way his mother sat outside his bedroom door that Howard went back downstairs without even asking what was going on. For the first time he noticed how cold the house was, as though someone had left all the windows open. He was about to turn on a light when he heard his mother say, "I'll go ahead and call Dr. Skinner now and have him come over. Sometimes you feel better if you talk it out with someone when you're . . . upset about something. So I'll just go downstairs now and give Dr. Skinner a call, OK?"

He realized she was talking to Walter, that Walter was somewhere in the dark room, listening, and he wondered if they'd been at each other all afternoon. He wanted to run, but he couldn't think of anywhere to go, so he went back into the kitchen and sat at the table without turning on the light.

His mother appeared shortly and leaned up against the doorway as if it were the first time in a long time she'd had a rest. She crossed her arms and shook her head and looked at Howard.

"Your brother's had some bad news. Word came this afternoon. He's going to Vietnam. He's . . ." Her voice trailed off, and she shook her head again. "He's not taking it very well."

Howard pushed past his mother on his way upstairs, but she put her hand on his arm. "I think he wants to be alone now, Howard." Her face brightened, and she said, "I know what let's do. What do you say you go out and get us all some hamburgers at Steak 'n' Shake. I haven't had time to do anything about supper, and, well, I'm just dying for a good cheeseburger and a chocolate malted. What do you say?"

Howard looked his mother square in the face and turned towards the stairs.

"Howard," she said, "please. Don't go up there." She grabbed for his shirt sleeve, but he pulled away and kept on walking. "Howard," she said in a sharp, raspy whisper, "I'm afraid."

So was Howard, but he decided he wanted to see for himself what was going on, so he kept on walking, turning on lamps as he went. When he turned one on in the living room, he noticed the drapes were being sucked out the open windows, but the windows weren't open; they were broken—every single one of them.

Howard turned on all the lights in the living room and then the dining room and his mother's bedroom. Walter must have smashed every window in the whole house. He ran up the stairs, taking them two at a time, and when he got to their bedroom door, he reached in and flipped the light switch.

Walter sat on the floor. He wore his military camouflage fatigues. He sat with his back against the wall underneath a broken window, and he held the shotgun aimed at Howard's head. They were still for a moment, looking at each other. Walter raised the gun higher, so it was aimed at the ceiling. His eyes had a look in them that reminded Howard of a field mouse he'd found once in the kitchen trash. It had crawled into an empty cellophane bag and was trying to scratch its way through the plastic because it was running out of air.

Right after the gun went off and shot out the light fixture, Howard heard his mother cry and make her way to the phone.

"Walter," he said into the dark. "It's me, Howard. Grab your jacket and let's get out of here. Mom's calling the police."

Howard heard Walter move and watched his dark form rise in front of the window. He didn't know which way the gun was pointed, and he worried about this, but he didn't move until Walter was standing next to him in the doorway. He hadn't picked up a jacket. Howard warned him that it was cold and then figured it was a waste of time to haggle over it. Walter was tough. The Marines taught you how to survive in the wild without a jacket. They taught you how to live on snake meat and weeds. Walter had described it again and again, but it was only now that Howard realized he hadn't been bragging. Not exactly. He had sounded angry and sarcastic, and it occurred to him that Walter had been scared all along—scared shitless.

Howard turned and ran down the stairs and heard Walter following him. He didn't know where he was leading him, but he kept on going through the kitchen, and Walter was right behind him. They ran hard once they were out the back door, and because Walter was in far better shape, he pulled out ahead of Howard, who had to struggle to keep up. Howard was suddenly afraid of losing his brother, afraid Walter would keep on running. He could see Walter's body, arms pumping, head down, running through the tall dead grass as they made their way across the Kennedys' back meadow. Howard wanted to shout, "Stop! Wait for me!" And yet his whole purpose had been to help Walter to escape.

But now, as they headed toward the woods, the dark widened and stretched out between them, and the connection Howard felt to his brother thinned and would snap any second. Because it was so thin, he knew it could break, and if it broke, it would be gone forever. He wanted to stop him, to hold on to him, to make sure wherever they went, they'd go together, and even as he realized this, he stopped running, could feel the thread break in his own chest, and as he stood still, listening to the high-pitched throb of a police siren from somewhere behind him, he called out, "Walter," just once, and watched his brother leap over a pile of mud and disappear into the dark woods.